No Holding Back

By

D. E. Arrington

ISBN 0-7414-3397-4

Published by:

INFIN∞ITY
PUBLISHING.COM

1094 New DeHaven Street, Suite 100
West Conshohocken, PA 19428-2713
Info@buybooksontheweb.com
www.buybooksontheweb.com
Toll-free (877) BUY BOOK
Local Phone (610) 941-9999
Fax (610) 941-9959

Printed in the United States of America

Printed on Recycled Paper

Published September 2006

Acknowledgments:

Thank you to all of those who truly believed in me even when I doubted myself. Thank you to my Lord and Savior, Jesus Christ, through faith in him all things are possible and faith has a meaning.

I want to thank my mother Patricia Crawford, for being there and for passing on your creative genes to me. To my loving and devoted husband Michael: this is just the beginning and thank you for just being you.

To Lauren, Mr. Beasley, Dionne, Abby, Nikki P., and Mom Arrington: thank you for reading this even when it had all the typos in the world and offering sound feed back.

Thank You, Renee Biggs for the wonderful cover art: you are truly gifted.

To Charleka, JaNale, Elizabeth, Nikki, Keisha and Timeka: thanks for listening, laughing, and crying with me even when it had nothing to do with this book.

To anyone not listed but not forgotten: thank you for your contributions, support, and unconditional love.

We did it yall!!!!

D. E. Arrington

For Michael, My Love

and For Lauren, My Motivator

Chapter One

He knew the moment he woke that his day was not going to go well. There was an eerie feeling all around him. Something wasn't right. Trying to focus his vision, he noticed the alarm clock flashing 3:04 am. The power must have gone out the night before, no telling what time it really was.

After spending what felt like forever but in reality was only a few seconds staring at the flashing clock, he retrieved his watch from the mahogany nightstand flanking the right side of his bed. 7:12. He'd over slept by almost forty-five minutes. Kicking the covers off his legs he jumped out of bed and started to rethink his day. A forty-five minute set back meant skipping breakfast and getting into the office early was beyond him knowing the traffic during rush hour in the winter months.

The ringing phone snapped him out of his early morning haze. He rushed to the phone and answered in the middle of the third ring.

"Hello"

"Al? What the hell is going on? I was starting to get worried. Did you forget about your early meeting?"

It was Al's assistant, Isabel. Actually he had forgotten about the meeting with his new client, he'd been forgetting a lot of things that involved work quite frequently; his father accused him of being distracted and unfocused. Al wouldn't go that far, but for some unknown reason he couldn't get himself together.

"Shit! Bel, I did forget. Can he wait or reschedule for later today? The power in the building must have gone out and my alarm clock didn't go off. Shit, shit, shit!"

"I'm going to wash that mouth of yours out with soap. Anyway, I covered for you. He said that he'll meet you for dinner at John Q's for an early dinner at five"

"Thanks I owe you one"

"That's fine, but you owe me more than one, your tab is eighteen pages long and you don't pay me enough for the things you put me through. I can't figure out how you moved from the city that never sleeps and manage to over sleep"

Laughing Al replied, "I'm trying to catch up on all that I missed."

Isabel didn't laugh at his tacky attempt at humor but Al knew that she was smiling. Isabel Hartford wasn't the type to laugh but occasionally she would flash a smile that could light up a room. Isabel's attractiveness hadn't diminished over her forty-five years. Her burnt orange complexion and long wavy hair told of her Native American heritage. She'd related to Al once the story of her family heritage and how her African American father had fallen head over heals in love with her Navajo mother in college.

Al reminisced on how she came to him on the recommendation of one of his former clients now serving time for fraud. His client told him that Isabel was smart, articulate, and sneakier than the devil himself. Al figured that was more than likely the reason her former employer sat in jail and not her.

"Bel, tell me, isn't there a faster way into Downtown other than having to drive through the streets? Can't I take the highway or something?"

"Nope"

"Are you sure?"

"Yup"

"Positive?" her monocyclic answers grated on his nerves.

"Wouldn't had said so if I weren't." Letting out a frustrated sigh she continued. "Look, I've been living in this city all my life and I would tell you otherwise if there was an otherwise. Now be wise and get your tail in here before your Father notices"

He replied in a military mocking voice "Sir, yes sir!"

"Don't play with me" her voice was coated with irritation she continued, "Instead of fighting with traffic, weather, and parking, why don't you just take the train in?"

"How often does it run?"

"Every ten or fifteen minutes from the Square until about nine then it becomes every fifteen to twenty minutes."

"How much does it cost?"

"Buck fifty, exact change, don't have change, get some when you get off at the station."

"Alright then, I'll see you in an hour."

"Good-bye" Her closing words always sounded as if she were singing. It was as if she wanted to end every conversation on a good note, literally.

Al showered, dressed, and reset the clock in his bedroom before he pulled out his planner and checked and rearranged some of the meetings in it. He'd call Sam later and change their plans to go to dinner and meet her after his dinner meeting. At 7:50am Al walked out of his apartment building and made a quick right turn onto Shaker Boulevard towards the rapid station.

****

Al had no clue that he would look so out of place when he dressed that morning. One not paying attention to the person standing closest to them is a normal thing in the Big Apple but not in Cleveland. In Cleveland everyone notices everyone. If one isn't from around there, it's almost as bad as being the only boy at a cheerleading competition, they stick out. Al had put on his black Hugo Boss suit with the pewter toned buttons, Blue shirt, blue and white stripped tie with dark gray accent pin-stripes, his favorite also from Hugo Boss, and his favorite lace up Kenneth Cole's.

It was beyond Al that people in Cleveland wore sensible winter attire or at the very least shoes that matched the weather, especially when they caught public transportation.

Standing there in what would be a normal thing back home he felt the eyes of people who were not exactly looking at him but not exactly oblivious to his presence. It wasn't as if it didn't snow in New York but there, the subway was no more than a block from home or he could just step out of his apartment and hail a taxi. In Cleveland however; things ran differently. It's a life of less convenience. People around there worked hard for everything they had including a ride to work. It was a life that Al respected and admired. No matter that his parents had financial wealth, he wanted little to do with it and made a point of working for all that he had accumulated.

Al had a look about him that stood out to passers by. He fit the preverbal 'tall, dark, and handsome' mold. A few inches over six feet, hair as dark a brown that it toyed with being black, and eyes the color of an indigo blue glass bottle. He looked too clean and handsome to be from around town and everyone at the rapid station knew it.

The rapid arrived at 7:58. Al missed it. He was on the wrong side of the tracks.

Chapter Two

Veronica stood in line at the Diner and watched the stranger lost in a new land miss his train, she figured that he missed his train because he stood there as two went by him going in the direction that he should have gone on that side of the tracks with out boarding either. He looked cold and irritated. No hat, no gloves, no scarf. He had on a long black wool overcoat, nothing else, just him, his suit, his overcoat, and the blistering cold.

Typical Cleveland weather in November is cold, not as cold as January or February, but very cold none the less, and if one is from Cleveland they are pretty much used to it. It's another day at the park. When the temperature hit 15 or 20 degrees an extreme weather warning may pop up. If it happens to stay just above freezing it's the middle of a heat wave. Veronica loved the fall and the winter, couldn't decide which she adored the most. However, seeing this man protect his pride made Veronica shiver. He looked like either he wasn't accustomed to the weather or he wasn't accustomed to taking the public transportation in this city.

It was cold this day. No snow, just really cold. It hadn't snowed in about three days so most of the streets and sidewalks were clear, but with the low temperatures and freezing rain there were spots of black ice. Black ice is a driver's worst nightmare, the ground looks wet, but it's not. It's a thin layer of ice on the asphalt that has been the cause of car accidents, people falling on their rear sides while walking, and everything involving the lack of traction.

Veronica made it to the counter of the diner, after the elderly lady who resided in the building next door to her own preached to the owner about the virtues of being saved by the blood of Jesus.

"Lady, lady! I Greek! Okay! I not from Afghan! Go! You hold up my line! Go! Okay"

"Okay, but last night I had me a dream that you ain't no Christian, I know you ain't. God will help you see. Go to God. Go to God"

The diner owner had a look of desperation in his eyes. Veronica knew the elderly woman harassing him. What she didn't know was how a woman three times her age managed to walk the short block to the diner to play the lottery without falling and needing an ambulance. Maybe God was on her side.

Veronica decided to step in and help out Tony the diner owner.

"Mrs. Payton, why are you giving Mr. Tony here a hard time? He's always nice to you and plays your numbers."

"Why you in my bizzness gal?" a near by Patron stopped eating to watch the scene unfold.

"Cause I don't wanna miss my train, if that is alright with you." Veronica replied sweetly.

The old woman took a moment to assess Veronica. She gave Veronica the standard stare down, one of trying to let Veronica know that she thought her smaller than herself. The whole diner was watching now, all unsure of what was going to happen next. Everyone wanted to see if Mrs. Payton would try and make things physical, and knowing her that wasn't an absurd idea. Mrs. Payton's face showed the lines of thought. She was doing more than assessing the young lady standing in line behind her, but more trying to figure out how she was going to come out the situation looking like a dignified woman.

Her memory had become more fleeting by the day and she was a lot more testy than normal. Her doctor had been telling her that she needed to drink red wine and green tea to help keep her memory going, but she wasn't fooled, the Alzheimer's was becoming worse by the day. Soon her independence that she worked so hard for would be gone like her memory. It was time for her to make an exit, but she didn't know how to do so without coming off looking like a fool.

Veronica could tell that the woman was embarrassed. Tony saw the emotion written all over the senior's face. Tony was the first to speak.

"Okay, one day I go with you. You show me Jesus. Change my life. Okay?"

"Okay." Mrs. Payton answered. She flashed a sincere smile, did a false fixing of her hair, and turned to walk out the door.

Tony gave Veronica a brief smile that was mixed with gratitude and relief.

"Ronnie, thank you. Third time this week she come in like that. What's wrong with her? She's not taking her medication"

"I think you're right Tony. I'll talk to her granddaughter later today and ask her to check in on her."

Veronica went to the coffee station and made two cups and placed her money on the counter to pay for them as she always does, and as always Tony gave her a look of displeasure. He began reprimanding her "You know better, you no pay for anything. I tell you all time, you no pay…"

Veronica placed her hand up to signal for Tony to stop and began to explain herself . "Tony it's all right. I have two cups see I'm paying for somebody else's." She gave him a half smile, then in her best accent she imitated Tony "I no pay, I no pay."

Tony appreciated her humor but was still concerned about her paying for anything. They shared a special kind of friendship that most didn't understand. Veronica's Mother had started working for Tony years ago when the diner had first opened for business. Everyday when Veronica would leave school she would catch the train to the diner and wait for her mother to finish her shift.

The first time that she had ever tasted coffee was at his diner, she became hooked on it and had to have a cup of it at the beginning of her day, every day, and she always had it from the Diner. Her mother worked there for another five years until Veronica graduated from high school.

During that time Veronica and Tony had forged a relationship almost like father-daughter. He gave her advice, provided her mother and herself a place to stay when they were homeless and, during Veronica's toughest moments in life it was always Tony who provided a shoulder for her to lean on. Sometimes he was the only person she could trust. Not even her mother could help, like Tony had, when times were at their worst.

Tony saw Veronica as his own child. There was nothing in the world that he wouldn't do for her. The day she graduated from high school, he was there. When she graduated from college, he was in the front row. Veronica had no clue when he'd come to love her as he did, she just began to accept it. He was the closest thing that she had to a father. He was the strongest male influence in her life. He was her brother, her uncle, her father, and she truly loved him for it.

"Tony I gotta go, but I'll see you later. I'm off today so I'll stop in and help out a little." She loved coming in and helping his staff out. She liked his workers and she really like the hospitality and warm feeling that she got from working in the diner.

"Okay you go. I'll ask later who other coffee for. Huh?" He gave her a questioning look.

"It's nothing like that Tony, you see that man on the other side of the tracks? It's for him"

"Who is he?"

"I don't know. He looks cold." She said with a casual shrug.

"No look, he is cold. Be careful."

"Alright." She said with a laugh, enjoying the fatherly concern that was laced in his voice. "I'll see you later." Veronica walked behind the counter, placed a quick kiss on Tony's cheek and walked out of the diner towards the man on the wrong side of the tracks.

****

"I think you're standing on the wrong side," it sounded more like a question than the general statement it was intended to be. Veronica cautiously walked towards the handsome young man and extended her right hand that held the steaming hot cup of regular coffee.

Al looked at the young lady who seemed to be handing him a peace offering, however, no war lines had been drawn between them. He thought for a moment and decided that she was extending good ol' fashioned Ohio hospitality to help him. It was cold outside and he was the frost's captive. He accepted the coffee and took a long sip from the Styrofoam container letting the caffeine seep into his system and warm him.

"I figured that out a train ago. I didn't like the way the people on the other side were looking at me so I decided to wait"

"Look" she said and took a pause to take a moment to enjoy the dark hot liquid that was in her hand. "People look at you all the time, and they'll probably look at you for the rest of your life" especially if you continue to look that good, she added to herself. "Anyways" she continued "you don't strike me as someone who's insecure."

"Usually I'm not. But today it seems the cold has gotten the best of my judgment"

"Fair enough. Although I do suggest that we move to the other side of the tracks because a train is coming and I don't think that either of our days will start on time if we miss it" Al followed the young lady across the tracks and to the waiting platform for the northbound train.

Al was truly confused. What did this woman want from him? No one just walked up to you and offered coffee. At least that's not something he would do. Albeit he was thankful for the beverage, but he was sure that the young lady should save her money and not spend it on him. She didn't look poor but she certainly wasn't a glamour queen.

9

He found himself looking the young woman over. She had beautiful medium brown skin, even in the harsh, dry winter weather. It reminded him of a milk chocolate bar. She couldn't have been more than five foot five or six inches tall, with dark but clear eyes. Her eyes said there were many layers to her but those layers were honest. He could instantly tell by looking into those nut brown orbs that she wore her emotions on her sleeve. She had some weight to her frame, probably a healthy size twelve, not his usual preference, but it fitted her. His eyes wondered to her feet, that was his money meter. She wore a pair cheap knock off rugged outdoor boots. The kinds that are made to look like a new pair of Timberlands but in fact came from a chain store that didn't have a pair of shoes over $40.

Her voice interrupted his train of thought. "What was that?" he asked.

"I said that you're obviously not from around here, I can tell by your clothes, and I was wondering where you're from? Someplace warmer I suspect."

"You suspect wrong," he snapped back. He wasn't sure why he had caught such an attitude with her. He thought that maybe it was the chill outside that was making him bitter inside but once he thought about it he realized what it was; she made an assumption about him.

Assumptions being made on his behalf were his pet peeve and he certainly didn't appreciate them coming from someone whom he just met. Maybe the coffee was a peace offering; he just didn't know the war had started already he thought to himself. "Didn't mean to offend you! Sorry!" He felt a small amount of guilt tug at his heart when he saw the hurt that his response caused in her eyes. She does ware her emotions on her sleeves he thought to himself.

Veronica couldn't figure out why he lashed out at her and she certainly wasn't going to risk him doing it again. She made a quick resolve to cut the conversation short and not to sit near him on the train. When the train pulled up and came to a complete stop Veronica looked at the stranger holding an almost empty cup of coffee, *when did he drink it*

10

all, and said a polite good-bye, wished him well on his day, and boarded the train.

Instantly Al felt like the biggest jackass this side of the universe. Not only did he accept the coffee from the young woman, he didn't even show gratitude towards her, and to make matters worse he took his frustrations out on her.

Al felt compelled to make amends for his lack of civility. He wanted to apologize for his actions but the young lady had already ascended the steps on the train and expertly found and settled into a seat next to someone she apparently knew. Al knew he had messed up but there was really nothing he could do about it in the here and now. The people on the train were unforgiving with space and Al felt that it was an inopportune time. He made the resolve that he would catch her Down Town, if she de-boarded, He'd pull her to the side and express his regret for his outburst.

Chapter Three

Guilt became Al's worst enemy. The past two weeks had been horrible for him. He was having trouble with contractors; he couldn't find a suitable way to advertise, and his meeting with Mr. Dirthings was a complete wash up. Not to mention, he never got the chance to apologize to the young lady for his cruel remark. Even two weeks after the incident, he couldn't banish the thought of guilt from his mind. He had no clue why he was so bothered that he had upset a complete stranger, he wouldn't have cared had he been back in the North East. Then again, back there, the incident probably wouldn't have happened. No one pays that much attention to another in New York. They don't get offended easily either. On any given day, one can be insulted, yelled at, stabbed, shot, or any other horrible thing one could think of and its business as usual.

That's not to say New Yorkers are horrible, insensitive, unfeeling people, anyone who can remember the tragedy of September 11th is a living testimony of the opposite. New York City is a different place, most love it, some hate it, and no one has lived till they visit there. However if one is a native of or spent a long time in the Apple, then they look and react to most things differently than people from Cleveland.

Maybe I'm starting to become one of them. Al thought to himself as he looked over the cost projections for the kitchen equipment. That had to be the only logical explanation as to why he felt so horrible for snapping at the young lady. In the half month that had passed he had tried to come up with any logical reason as to why he lashed out at her, the weather, him oversleeping, his meeting with Mr. Dirthings, none of them were the cause. He had gone so far as to examine the possibility of the cause being the young woman herself. Maybe her appearance, forthrightness, he even entertained that maybe it was because she was black.

Isabel had made sure to dash that train of thought and that he didn't continue with it once he told her the whole situation.

"Bel, I'm telling you. I don't have a problem with African Americans. If I did I don't think I would be talking to you, hell I wouldn't have hired you in the first place."

"My race had nothing to do with it. You had no choice in hiring me, you helped put my boss in jail remember?" Isabel and her former employer were close, but she knew that he was misleading his clients and she also knew that Al was out to teach him a lesson especially when his misleading involved his family.

"Sure I had a choice. I could have hired that big-breasted blonde, but I didn't. I hired the right person for the job. Besides you came with glowing references."

"Of course I did! I helped him beat half the charges while I helped the prosecutor gather some pretty deep shit on him. Anyone who does that and can still sleep at night deserves at the very least a new job."

Al reminisced to when his parents first found out that Ivan Brown had scammed them out of $2.5 million. He was a private investor who was placing their money into a mixture of legit and false companies. The Carter's finally found out what was really happening when the family accountant looked at their portfolio about three months after the initial investments were made. Ivan was really clever with hiding the money, however Isabel turned out to be smarter. Not only had she made sure that she virtually didn't exist when it came to Brown Investment's Inc., she began making, keeping, and occasionally anonymously supplying the authorities with copies of some very precious paperwork that was supposed to have been destroyed.

The Carter's received a small portion of their initial investments back but still lost a huge amount of money. Al wasn't really upset with Ivan for swindling his parents. They should have been more careful with that kind of money. Besides the whole situation allowed him to acquire one of the best personal assistants in the city and it allowed his parents to finally convince Al to move to Cleveland and be closer to them.

It was dark outside but not very late by the time Al left his office on West Sixth and began his journey home. He was starting to enjoy his short commutes on the rapid to and from the office. His true hope was to maybe run into the coffee lady, that was what he called her since he didn't know her name, and possibly try to talk to her and convince her that he was a civil person. He had no such luck. Some days he would see a woman with her shape but once she would turn around he discovered that she was too dark, or too light, or in one case not even black.

Once he reached Tower City Mall Al's cell phone started vibrating. After checking to see if it was business or personal he answered the call. Al made it a point not to talk to people affiliated with work once he left work unless it was an emergency; he had a pager for emergencies.

"Hey Babe!" he greeted his somewhat girlfriend Samantha Riley. Al and Samantha had been occupying each other's free time without invading each other's space for the past few months.

"Hey yourself." She said in a sultry timber, which indicated that she meant to get some time in with Al.

"Uh oh! I know what that tone means"

"Well…since you've mentioned it?" She let the statement hang more like a question. Sam had a way of convincing people that they want to do something that they probably had no intentions of in the first place. She was attempting this ploy with Al. However she had no clue that he wasn't in a convincing mood. He just wanted to get some of his Christmas shopping done and head home. He had a day full of interviews ahead of him and he was going to need

14

to look over all of the potential's resumes and applications before the night was over.

"I didn't mention anything to be honest with you. However I'm going to turn down your offer. I have a lot of work to do tonight and I really don't feel like having to drive all the way over to the west-side to see you."

"How do you know I didn't want to come to see you?" Her voice loaded with disappointment.

"Because I know you, you hate the east side and you hate driving to the east side even more." Al could imagine Sam twirling a lock of her natural red hair; she had a habit of doing so when she was thinking of a way to get what she wanted when the first option didn't pan out.

"Al..." She had settled on whining.

"Sam, forget it. You know I loathe whining so don't even start."

"Well, you can't blame me for trying."

"I most certainly can. Blame implies that you knew exactly what you were doing before you did it, and you my dear are the most calculating woman I've ever known." That was one of the qualities that had attracted Al to Sam. She had a way of getting what she wanted from anyone without shedding an ounce of womanly appeal. She never had to degrade herself for anything and lying wasn't part of her repertoire. Sam just made a habit of only telling the truth that needed to be told when it needed to be told.

"Enough with the banter! Are you going to come by or what?" She also had a way of taking control of a situation when she became annoyed. She only became annoyed when a situation did not go the way she wanted.

"No, I'm not." His answer held a tone finality and sternness, firmness that Sam could detect instantly and that made her burn with desire for him. She enjoyed the challenge that a refusal to share her bed posed. She reveled in her desire to play cat and mouse and never caring which role she would play for the day. Cats got the opportunity to chase, seek, and ravage the spoils of the hunt; while the mouse has the advantage of seeing the hunter for what it is, hungry, greedy, and more times than not blinded by the thrill of the chase.

"Well in that case, I'm not going to hold you."

"Good." Not wanting to play into any more of her games, Al felt the need to end the call.

"Shall I see you Saturday?" She inquired.

"As planned."

"Well… I guess I could let you go…" She was stalling for time and Al was beginning to become annoyed with her tactics.

"Uh, Sam, is there a reason why we are still on the phone?"

"No, there isn't. Good-bye." The line went dead. Al drew the conclusion that Sam wasn't in the mood to let him get in a last word much less a polite farewell. All that withstanding he had the confidence to know that they would still see each other as scheduled on Saturday.

****

"I've told you a million times, and this makes a million and one. I don't have time for a man right now."

"Well I just can't see any reason as to why not. You've completed college, maintained a job while establishing a career. The only thing left for you to do is find a good man and start making me some grandbabies."

Veronica's patience had worn paper- thin with the all too familiar conversation that was taking place between her and her mother. Tammy Parker felt that her daughter had spent far too much of her life hiding behind academics, family obligation, and career building.

"Ronnie, listen to me will you. You didn't go to prom, never went on a date, never brought home a boy and, never showed any interest in dating. Are you gay?"

"I can't believe you." Veronica said in awe of her mother's candor. Her mother had a habit of always speaking her mind regardless of the consequences but Veronica believed that Tammy could take things to far at times.

"And if you recall, I did date a boy for a while, remember?"

"Yeah, I remember, but that was almost ten years ago. You were what 15? Anyway, I just think that you need to get out more." Tammy was always concerned that her daughter seemed to be too anti-social.

"I get out just fine. I have lots of social events that I attend and I am active at the church. Really, Ma, I just can't see me getting involved with anyone right now. I've got a lot on my plate and I enjoy it that way."

"Alright! I'll leave it be for now but, I will bring it up again."

"I'm so sure you will."

"Don't get smart with me!"

"Do I ever get sassy with you?" Veronica playfully asked with a coy grin.

"Always!" Tammy adored her only child. She had her at the age of sixteen and never had one regret for doing so. During her pregnancy she swore that she would raise her child to be proud of who she was and where she came from, she had succeeded well beyond her expectations.

"So what time will you have my car back to me?" Tammy inquired. Veronica believed that she and the giver of her life shared a bond that extended beyond the perimeters of mother and child. She believed that her mother was the one who held her secrets. Even in the time that she couldn't turn to her mom, she knew that Tammy Parker possessed knowledge about her daughter that not even she could explain the acquisition.

"I should be able to pick you up from work. It shouldn't take all day. I believe that I'm the last candidate to go in; however I have the least experience and I'm coming in under the hopes of the program, so by the time they get to me the choice will probably have already been made"

"You think so?" Tammy couldn't believe that her daughter would doubt her talents, but now wasn't the time to

17

mention this thought. If Tammy knew anything about her daughter she knew that her ego was fragile and even when one tries to be helpful and boost it, she wound up being less confident.

"Yeah I do. I mean I have a lot of experience in the hospitality field, some food and beverage, but I don't think it's enough. Even with my degree in business and the backing of the program I don't think that they're looking for young, female, and black. This is a big project and it just screams mid-thirties white male." Veronica looked at herself as a realist. And reality said that she had a commitment to the people who've invested in her to interview for this position, but she wasn't going to get the job. To her that was reality. Reality went by rules and not hopes. Dreams kept her hungry; reality put food on her table. The reality was she could probably do the job better than anyone of her competitors, but it also said that she wouldn't have even gotten this far in the process without the help of influential people. That was reality at its best.

"Alright then, I guess I should see you at about six?"

"Yeah maybe before depending on how everything goes."

"See you later baby. I love you and good luck."

"I love you to, and thanks for having so much faith in me."

"It's the most natural thing for me to do."

Veronica pulled away from the curb with a resolve to make her mother proud of her. Looking at her mother waving at her in the rearview mirror Veronica squared her shoulders a little more and made a promise to her self. She decided as she approached the stoplight that from that point on the lights in her life would always be green.

****

The CaSa offices drove home the fact that they possessed wealth that the family was well known to have, or at least that was the impression Veronica got while sitting in the lobby. The impression made upon her was that the company made its money by being extremely smart with it in the end. It was obvious that the furnishings weren't inexpensive however, they weren't elaborate.

The color scheme put one in the thought of the Roman Empire complete with blinding white window treatments. The simplicity of it gave an air of calm and quiet but the intricately designed marble flooring with gold accents was not lost on Veronica's perceptive eye. This business was the epitome of comfortable luxury.

Veronica had an appreciation for people who didn't flaunt their apparent fortune, but made a statement in an understated way. She would prefer an intimate gathering of friends and family with good food and drink to bring in the New Year, as opposed to lavish over-indulgence displayed to the public in the tabloids. In her few years on earth, Veronica had opportunities to assimilate into the world of the indulgent lifestyle; however she couldn't bring herself to abandon her value system for another.

"Ms. Parker, Mr. Carter will see you now." The middle-aged receptionist spoke to Veronica breaking her trance. Veronica bent down to grab her back-pack styled purse and stood up. She was on wobbly knees and she hoped that her nervousness didn't show.

"Calm down sweetheart, this isn't the principal's office. He won't bite." So much for appearing calm, Veronica thought to herself.

"Thank you." She tried to smile but felt unfamiliarly nauseated and couldn't make her facial muscles form the pleasant gesture. Instead she came out looking as if she were in a great deal of pain. *Get it together girlfriend,* she told herself. Veronica's nervousness surprised her and gave her a feeling of incapability. It was a feeling that she didn't like and she wished it would go away at that very instant.

"…She'll be to your office in just a moment." The receptionist spoke into the phone while keeping her mother hen gaze fixed on Veronica. After finishing the short telephone conversation the receptionist rose out of her seat, rounded her desk, and grabbed Veronica by the arm and led her into the private restroom, where Veronica quickly entered the stall and discarded her lunch. Upon exiting the newly christened stall the receptionist quickly saw to attending to Veronica's appearance. She had produced a wet cloth and began wiping down her face, she had searched through Veronica's make-up case and laid the needed items out on the counter, and she had recovered some breath mints from only God knew where.

Veronica stared at the older woman in amazement. The woman didn't say a word but went about her business of making Veronica look presentable for her interview.

"I must be coming down with something, I mean why else would I be in here losing my lunch. I want to thank you for getting me in here in time to save the flooring. Oh my God! What am I going to do, this can't present a good picture of me to Mr. Carter..." Veronica was babbling.

"I took care of everything." The woman interrupted,

"But I..." She began in protest.

"But nothing child, this is probably the most important thing that you have done so far in your life and you will not mess it up on my watch." The receptionist's tone was saturated with finality and Veronica would have been a fool to continue in defense.

"You're right." She agreed breathlessly.

"Of course I am, now you get your tail in there and do what you do. Don't take no for an answer, and keep a level head about your self." The woman braced her hands on Ronnie's upper arms and quirked her right brow in an "any more questions" gesture. Veronica shook her head in submission, broke loose of the woman's hold and fixed her clothing.

"I can do this." She said aloud but not for the intentions of an audience. "I can do this." She repeated along with releasing a long breath. Never in her life had she been nervous for an interview of any kind. When she was thirteen and was going for a spot in the Initiative, when she was sixteen and interviewed for the position at the library, when she was interviewed by the local paper for the charity ball, or when she had the most intensive and personal question and answer session with her Doctor, never had she felt what she was experiencing right now. This was something new to her; this was a true test of her competency and she hated the feeling of unworthiness that had consumed her because of it.

Chapter Four

His cologne greeted her the second she entered the expansive office. His head was down and he was paying close attention to the document lying on his desk. He was so consumed into his work that he hadn't noticed her walk in. She cleared her throat to announce her presence and nearly fainted when Al lifted his head and met her gaze. It was him. Since that day at the train station she couldn't stop thinking about him. She couldn't stop thinking about how he had snapped at her after she'd spent a dollar of her to hard to come by money on him, a complete stranger, and he treated her like dirt. She couldn't stop thinking how helpless and vulnerable he was prior to her trying to be kind to him, and how aloof he'd become the second he got himself situated. She couldn't help but think about how somehow he had made her feel like less than nothing with the speaking of a few words coated in privilege, directed to her mediocre being.

However, at that very moment all she could think about was how she would love to gouge out the most beautiful blue eyes she'd ever seen.

The shock in Al's eyes was obvious. He hadn't thought that he'd see the coffee yielding young woman ever again and certainly not in an interview situation. He wasn't sure how to handle this turn of events. The only thing he was sure of was at that very moment she was a stunning vision. She wasn't his normal type of woman but that with standing, she was even more beautiful than he had remembered. She stood glaring at him but that didn't change the fact that she had the most elegantly shaped eyes and the down turn of her mouth made the heat in his body turn up. Although she was thicker in body, there was a womanly appeal drenched in the curves of its form. Far from skinny, she looked as though she had hours of pleasure to give hidden in every curve. The thin long braids she wore were wavy and neatly pulled into a pony- tail. Her make-up was limited to lipstick and the gray suit she had on impaled and made one recognize her confidence. It was the snug fitting turtleneck, however; that made Al recognize the swell of her bosom. She was breath taking from the top of her head to tips of her boot-clad feet.

"Mrs. Winston told me to come in." She said apologetically. Why am I making excuses to him, she thought to herself, I have a right to be here. She gave him an expectant look as if to question if he were going to sit there muted or if he were going to remember his manners and invite her in. He spoke his answer to her silent question. "Yes please, won't you come in?" He rose out of his wingback chair, rounded his desk, and extended his hand. Veronica gathered her resolve then proceeded to perform as if the two had never met previously. Extending her hand Ronnie gave the handsome young man a polite smile and formally introduced her self. "Thank you, I'm Veronica Parker. It's a pleasure meeting you Mr. Carter."

The redness that had risen to Al's face was not lost on Veronica. She had presumed that it was because he had remembered her from two weeks prior and was now caught in an awkward predicament. Her observation was partially correct, however; she couldn't imagine the real reason behind his crimson flush cheeks.

"Well I wish that were a true statement Ms. Parker, but I don't recall it being such a pleasure two weeks ago." Until he had made that comment Veronica hadn't noticed that they yet to release from each others grasps. She smoothly removed her hand from his warm grip and mocked confusion. She had no intentions of giving this man another reason to believe that he had gotten under her skin. She'd chastised herself more than once since the encounter for letting him know the first time.

"I'm sorry, you seem to have me at a disadvantage." She blinked rapidly for effect.

"Surely you remember?"

"Remember what Mr. Carter?" She could have gotten an Oscar for the performance that she was putting on and it began to grate on Al's nerves.

"Remember what?" He repeated. It was clear to Veronica that he was at a lost for control over the situation and she was enjoying every second."

"Yes, what am I supposed to remember?"

"Two weeks ago, the rapid station, the cup of coffee?" He had to stop himself from raising his voice. He couldn't believe that she didn't remember the encounter. It wasn't as if she'd been unaffected; the memory of her hurt attacked his dreams at night.

"Oh yes that's right. I hope that you've learned to dress more appropriately for the weather since then." She retorted with laughter in her voice but not in her eyes. Al wasn't sure what he saw in her eyes but it wasn't pleasure. The only thing he was sure of at that moment was Veronica was an excellent actress, a quality needed in the industry. He liked her style already. Even though she'd been placed in a tough situation from the beginning, he had yet to see her sweat. Purposely, he'd set up the telephone interviews and initial meetings with his brother, Simon. Then, he'd conduct the final interview. This way no one could be too comfortable and think that just because they had a few experiences with one person that the position was theirs. Finally, he'd have the candidate wait a little longer than normal to be seen. It was his way of sorting out the calm and collected versus those who can't stand to have their cages rattled. Veronica seemed to have the calm and collected category under wraps. It was Al's nerves that were now on edge.

"Yes I have thank you. Please, have a seat over here." He led her to the sitting area of his office. His office was a complete contrast to the cool understated ambiance of the lobby. CaSa owned the turn of the century building but only utilized two floors and rented the rest. The remaining was utilized for anything from a doctor's office to a bail bondsman. The main lobby housed only a directory, security desk, and a few telephone booths. The lobby to the CaSa offices was cool and clear but the office of the young Mr. Carter was warm and fuzzy. Veronica felt like curling up on the sofa in the sitting area and opening a book.

Breaking the comfortable silence that had mysteriously engulfed the air between them, Al began the interview. "So Miss Parker, from the information that has been passed on to me from Simon, you are very familiar with our company, when did you first hear about us?" He wanted to understand how a perspective client or employee felt about CaSa. He'd been working for his Father since before he went to Cornell University. He'd been in love with the family business for as long as he could remember. CaSa was the largest restaurant and nightclub developer in the region, third largest in the country, and fifth in the world. The company specialized in developments in growing cities opposed to larger more established markets.

That didn't mean that the company didn't operate in larger cities, as a matter of fact, the home office is located in Manhattan. Al's parents had moved to Cleveland, Simon Sr.'s childhood home, to open and operate the office after they had sent Al to college twelve years prior.

"Well" Veronica began "As you know I am one of the original participants in the Initiative program." She met his gaze and for the first time Al noticed a softening in the brown orbs that showed honesty, sincerity, and reflection. They revealed a side of Veronica that Al was drawn to; a side of her he had to know more about. Without verbally interrupting her, Al coaxed the story along by nodding his head and assuming a non-threatening posture by keeping his arms on the rests of the chair and his legs crossed in a relaxed manner. Veronica took in all of his virile manhood and it made her insides burn. She made a mental note that Al Carter was very practical. He did nothing without careful thought. She could tell that his posture was trained; his eye contact intentional and his listening skills were acquired through some form of trial and error.

"I started in the program more than ten years ago during my freshman year in high school and since then I have become part of an extended family. That family includes those who have contributed to my growth. It includes those who have helped the program and in turn did me a great justice. CaSa is a part of that group."

"How so?" He asked.

"Well, when the Initiative was in financial trouble about six years ago due to cut backs from supporters, CaSa stepped in as an anonymous donator." She stated matter-of-factly. The look on her face denoted that she'd presumed his knowledge of the donation. His knowledge of such had been void until that moment. "You didn't know?" The rampage of thoughts played on his face and broke the rehearsed cool demeanor that he'd successfully displayed.

"I'm sorry. I assumed that you knew." She offered.

"You seem to have a habit of making assumptions, don't you Ms. Parker?" Al let all of his reserve slip. His dislike for others making assumptions about him and his judgments started very early in his life, however, he thought he had learned to control his feelings regarding the subject. He hadn't lost his temper about it in quite some time. That was before the incident at the train station. Some how, Veronica Parker got under his skin without any effort. She could make him unsure of himself.

"Excuse me Mr. Carter?" Veronica was a little put off by his comment, but she'd be damned if he was going to get her hairs up about it.

Not to be backed down by her, he repeated himself. Veronica couldn't believe that he had the audacity to say what he had the first time but she was in complete shock that he had the gall to actually say it twice. Her first thought was to let the sistah-girl in her come out and tell him about himself, his attitude, his assumptions, and where she personally felt like shoving them. The only thing that she knew that she couldn't do was to loose self control and let her emotions get the best of her, so rather than respond to his insult she placed a quaint if not pleasant smile on her face and proceeded as if the riff in the conversation never happened.

"Yes well..." clearing her throat she continued "The initiative has done a great deal of work in the community since it's inception and I am honored to have gone through their programs and now I am able to give back to the program by volunteering and mentoring. Experiencing the benefits of the program is one of the virtues of the Initiative that CaSa recognized six years ago." She could tell that she'd backed him into a corner. If looks could kill, her mother would have to come and identify the remains of her corpse.

He couldn't believe that she behaved as if he had said nothing to her. He had to admit that she had a way of not letting on if things get to her. Focus. She had focus, undeterred from the goal in front of her. Well if she was going to play that game so would he.

"Yes well, I'm glad that this company was able to help you." He eyed her trying to gage her reaction to his feigned impassiveness. She remained stoic. Continuing he said, "So please tell me more about yourself?" As Veronica began she relayed her phenomenal background in the hospitality field. She recounted her story of how the Initiative got her an internship at one of the leading hotels in the area and how from that point on she never looked back. She was able to finish high school a half year earlier than the rest of her class, something that Al made a mental note of seeing that he had graduated from high school at the age of sixteen. He had been born the gift of brains so being studious came easy, in fact came so easy that he never had to pick up a book or take notes to retain information. He wanted to test out of high school but his parents had refused, citing their insistence that he had as normal a childhood that they could give him. If he hadn't decided to go to law

27

school he would have obtained the three undergraduate degrees that bear his name in less than three years.

Their interview lasted a little more than an hour and a half and Veronica was starting to have some anxiety about ending the interview. She couldn't place her finger on it but for some reason she didn't want their exchange to end. She had to admit that Al Carter was an engaging debater and it didn't hurt his cause that he was drop dead gorgeous. She couldn't believe her thought pattern! She was actually imagining his full lips pressed against hers in unbridled passion. She could feel the warmth of his breath as it lingered by her ear. What she really wanted was to feel his elegantly large hands caress areas of her body that *she* hadn't acknowledged existed.

Veronica was so captivated by the man sitting across from her that she began to forget that she was there for business, something that she never lost sight of. Business was Veronica's first love and only love to be exact. She was enthralled by the lure of transactions and seduced by the gratification of a blissfully satisfied customer. She knew that business and more specifically the business of people and providing them with service was what she was destined for the moment she started her first job.

Freshman year of high school was intimidating for her; she was a year younger than her peers due to her skipping the first grade, however she felt removed from them beyond the age difference. At a very young age Veronica acquired wisdom, maturity, and composure that surpassed her station in life. The children in her fourth grade class became relentless in trying to make her feel inferior because of her superior wit. The teasing only became worse as she aged and it had become brutal and violent by the time she had reached high school. During freshman year she ate her lunch alone most of the time because her best friend was popular and chose to eat with the in fashion clique.

Her solitude didn't bother her as much as the fact that the sentence was inflicted upon her by someone else and the choice to be a loner was taken out of her control. Her personality left nothing to be desired. She was outgoing, friendly, and exquisitely polite. Her educators adored her and because of their admiration she was given the coveted position as the concession stand coordinator. Tradition dictated that the position be given to a qualified junior once they had successfully completed a year of working and mentoring under the departing senior. Veronica's demeanor and intelligence along with the misbehavior of the next successor earned her a more than sought after employment and her first taste of what would become her life's passion.

"It has been a pleasure talking with you Ms. Parker." He said rising to his feet and extending to his full six foot three inches height. He took a prolonged glance at his watch then turned his attention back to Veronica to find her on the floor. Not knowing what happened or what to do he stood there staring at her. Breaking his trance she yelled up to him "Help me up will you!" with a jerk he knelt down and placed his strong hands on her arms, shifted her from the face down position she was in to a sitting, and pulled her up to the love seat that she had just vacated.

Complete confusion marred his face. Veronica liked the stern outline of his jaw and his mouth had a delicate poutiness that bordered on feminine. *I wonder if he knows how good he looks. I wish I could lick his bottom lip. God he is beautiful. What? What the hell is wrong with me? Am I for real? Oh god he just peeled me off the floor and I'm thinking about licking lips and how he looks. Ugh!* Al saw the frown on Veronica's face and figured that it had some-thing to do with why she was on the floor face down. Speaking of which, how and why did she get down there? He asked as much and she replied "My leg. It fell asleep from having it crossed in the same position for such a long while"

"Why didn't you uncross them during the interview?"

"Because I didn't...I...I really don't know why." For the fist time since she had walked into his office Al was unable to put his acute awareness of Veronica Parker the curvaceous seductress aside and look at her as Veronica

Parker potential employee. Suddenly she stood and made a motion to step over his out stretched legs but her plans were foiled as her body betrayed her once again and her leg began to cramp. She toppled over onto his lap from the pain. Wincing she apologized and tried to move off his lap. With fluid motion and no effort, Al adjusted her position so that her legs were in his lap. Slowly he began to massage her right leg. Veronica tensed under his touch and Al could sense her uneasiness. She was as skittish as a frightened feline.

"Relax," he instructed just above a whisper.

"It's...um...it's the other leg." She stammered out.

"Okay." He gave a boyish grin as he gently moved his hand from one thigh to the next tracing his hand along the inside of the vacated leg. Veronica shuddered as his searing touch ignited a flame in her that she had no idea could even light up. Her leg was soft yet maintained a firmness that he wasn't accustomed to feeling on a woman. She gasped for air, as her chest felt restricted for the new heaviness that her breast seemed to attain. Al inched his hand further up her thigh. He knew that the encounter had already gone too far but he couldn't stop himself. The expression on her face egged him on. She went from a doe eyed innocent lamb to a purring feline relishing in the spoils of catching her prey.

Veronica licked her bottom lip and instantly regretted doing so. *Oh my God. Did I just do that? Yes, I did that and he actually looks like he liked it! Oh my God do I care what he likes. I want to work for this man not work the man. I gotta stop this but his hand ...feels...soooo...gooood!* Before Veronica could form another coherent thought Al took the situation to another dangerous level and covered her mouth with his. All resolve went out the window and Al moved his hands even more up her leg only to discover that she had been wearing a traditional garter instead of the full panty hose that many women chose to wear.

The discovery increased his interest and with that he increased the pressure of his kiss. He wasn't sure why but the response that he got from Veronica turned him on more. Veronica didn't part her lips for him; she simply applied more pressure and moved the muscles in her lips. He wanted more, much more, but he couldn't very well take her in his office. He just couldn't stop himself. She was splendid! He could tell that her experience with the opposite sex on an intimate level was limited for he felt like he was coaching her along instead her being his equal co-participant.

He forced his tongue into her mouth after nibbling on her bottom lip. Veronica's moan died in his throat as he began to make love to her mouth. Moving his hand from her legs he pulled off the band that was holding her hair in place and ran his fingers through the lengthy, skinny braids. He liked what he felt. Then almost as fast as his hands were in her hair he moved them back to the warm confines of her thighs. There his fingers pulled the satin covering of her panties to the side and began a slow methodic stroking of her pronounced love bud. Not once had he stopped kissing her, not once had she asked him to, nor did she want him to.

He could feel her overflow of moister tumble from the parted folds and it only made him want to explore more, excite her more, taste her more. He took a finger and inserted it into her soft feminine alcove and then inserted another while he busied his other hand with the task of grabbing her breast and fondling it until her nipple became rock hard. Veronica began to rock her hips against his soft-thrusting fingers as his thumb continued to tease her passion swollen nub and another gush of liquid threatened to scald Al's hand. He pulled away from their smoldering kiss. He wanted to watch her. Her face was flush and full of conflicting emotions, but she was to far gone to stop. Their gazes locked and the intensity of it all was Veronica's undoing. Arching her back and biting her lip to contain her screams of pleasure, Veronica closed her eyes and let the feeling of ecstasy take over. Al could feel her womanhood contract uncontrollably around his finger. Turning into the love seat Veronica felt as if she were at a cliff about to jump, then suddenly someone pushed her and that someone was Al

31

Carter. She heard a voice that she didn't recognize and soon realized it was her own. Then without warning, she exploded. A million tiny little pieces of glass, that's what her skin felt like. She called out for God several times before her convulsions simmered.

Al removed his fingers and then tasted his handy work from off them. That completely threw Veronica off kilter, but it didn't stop her from being turned on again. Al saw the hunger in her eyes but he also saw something that halted his breath, fear. Resolving to remove her fear he began a slow attack on her apprehensions and repeated the love making to her with his hand. By the end of the second round, Veronica was breathless and exhausted.

Chapter Five

Veronica walked into her apartment after returning from the gym, to find her best friend of fifteen years sitting on her sofa thumbing through the latest edition of a Hip Hop magazine. Veronica wouldn't have been so upset to see her but Renee didn't have a key to her place.

"What...how did you get in here?" Veronica questioned her confidant of more than half her life.

"What am I doing here? I haven't talked to you in a week and I wanna know how the interview went. How did I get in here? I waited in the lobby for an old lady to come through the security door then I just came up and picked the lock. You know you should have them insta..."

"Wait!" Veronica interrupted putting up her hand to signal Renee to stop speaking. Veronica was an only child to a teen parent while Renee was the youngest of four in a two parent middle class household. Their meeting had been one that wasn't in the cards for Renee. Seeing how Veronica was the official outcast for the whole sixth grade class, it was only fitting that no one wanted to sit next to her at the lunch table. One day; however, a new boy joined the class and seating became scarce at mealtime and Renee was forced to sit next to Veronica.

Renee was always forthright with her opinions even at the tender age of eleven. Veronica reminisced to that day, when Renee told her that she didn't appreciate having to sit next to the outcast nor would it become a regular occurrence. This day, as the young woman sat in her friends' living room, was no different. Veronica just wasn't up to her friends up front personality.

It had been a week since the interview and the incident after. Veronica had been avoiding her rambunctious friend for many reasons, the main one being she couldn't keep a secret from her if her life depended on it. The whole thing had Veronica shook up. She'd done something that she wasn't proud of, something that was unethical, improper, and down right wrong! She'd let a complete stranger, a potential employer perform an act on her that she had not willingly let another do.

"I'm so happy that you felt the need to prove your skills as a cat burglar, but do you think the next time you could do it at someone else's expense?" Cocking an eyebrow she crossed her arms and gave her friend a stern stare.

"What's the problem? It's not like you didn't expect me to show up!" Renee responded and went back to giving her attention to the magazine in her hands. Veronica gave an exasperated sigh, threw her hands in the air in an "I give up" manner, and turned and walked into her bathroom. "Where are you going?" Renee asked.

"To the bathroom. You gonna pick this lock too?" Veronica yelled through the closed door.

"No. I think I can wait for you to pee"

"Well you'll be waiting a little longer, cause I need a shower."

****

"You did what!?" Renee's jaw couldn't drop any lower. "He did what! You did what? What the hell were you thinking? *Were* you thinking? Wait, wait, wait, wait, waaaaiiit! I need to gather my thoughts, which, by the way, is what you should have done before you let your boss feel you up." After her semi-lecture to Veronica, Renee sat staring and blinking rapidly at her friend as if she had just sprouted a second head.

"Are you finished?" Veronica asked staring straight ahead at the television with her arms crossed over her chest. She didn't dare risk taking a look at her friend for she feared that she might loose her composure and break down. Her confidant was right. She'd screwed up, big time. What made matters worse was a Human Resources rep from the CaSa corporate offices called her the day before and offered her the Sales and Events Coordinator position. Reluctantly she accepted. She really had no choice. One, she was the long shot so if given the opportunity she had to take it, and two, she couldn't and wouldn't punk out. Just because she had one fleeting moment of poor judgment, didn't mean that she had to give up everything that she worked for.

"Ronnie? Ronnie, look at me." Renee pleaded.

"What?" Veronica replied rolling her eyes in the direction of her lecturer.

"I'm just freaking out. You haven't let anyone touch you much less do anything that …that serious to you in a long time. Hell you let one guy close to you, that didn't work out and it's been like you didn't acknowledge that you are a woman since." Renee recalled the whole ordeal that her best friend had to suffer. She'd always wondered if the situation had turned Veronica for the worse but never mentioned it to her. Renee had watched as Veronica suffered the humiliation of trying so hard to belong that she compromised her self-respect and the only thing that she came into this world with, her womanhood.

'I don't know what came over me. One minute I was cramping and sitting on his lap and the next he was kissing me and I was letting him and then it got out of control. Oh God what have I done?" Veronica was in a lot of pain. The anguish plastered on her face was evident to Renee.

Veronica was confused, plain and simple. There was no sugar coating it. While the circumstances that things had taken place were uncomfortable, the act in and of itself was grand. Veronica had never had the pleasure of a man being gentle, caring, and completely aware of her needs and wants. "Um Renee, there's more." Veronica confessed.

Renee shifted her position on the sofa so that she was completely facing Veronica. "How much more?" she asked.

"Well that depends on how you look at it. It could be considered a little under the circumstances, but I doubt that you'd see it that way." Veronica was a little apprehensive to give all the details especially given her friend's reaction to only hearing a small portion of the whole sordid event.

"Spill it!" Renee demanded.

"Well…" Veronica's thoughts trailed off back to that day at the office. After Al successfully made her his love slave by merely using his hands, he went to his private bathroom to freshen up. Veronica took this as her chance to escape. Once he had closed the door she righted her self, adjusted her clothing, and made a beeline for the door. She had made it to the elevator bank when Al caught up to her.

"Where do you think you're going?" His voiced barely above a whisper shook her to her core.

"The interview is over is it not Mr. Carter?" She'd surprised herself at how composed she sounded because she certainly did not feel it.

"I don't believe that it is Miss Parker." Al gave her a glare that told her everything she needed to know about Al Carter. He was very persuasive, demanding, and he played for keeps. He placed his hand on the small of her back, the slight touch made her shiver. After leading her back into his office he made a point to lock the door behind him. Without saying a word to her, Veronica watched as this man who withdrew from her what no other could, walk to his desk call his assistant and tell her that she didn't have to wait around for him to leave to close the office. He said that he would lock up everything and see that Miss Parker got to her car safely. What Veronica couldn't hear was Isabel's chastising of Al. There weren't many times that Isabel had pushed the line between employer and employee, but she felt the need tell him that not only had he pushed it that he had just blatantly trampled and rubbed it out as far as the young woman and he were concerned.

"Thank you Bel, I'll see you tomorrow." He said in closing.

"Yes you shall. Should I lock off the elevator?" She asked clearly searching for details as to how long he planned on being holed up in his office with the very attractive young woman.

"That will be fine; Miss Parker and I will utilize the stairs when we leave. Good night." He chanced a glance in Veronica's direction. She looked so tempting, she hadn't placed her hair back into the ponytail and it lay wildly on her shoulders. Her lips were still slightly swollen from extensive kissing, even though they needed nothing to make them fuller or more perfect in his eyes. He couldn't help but to smile at her, she had brought out something in him that no other woman could have, pure animalistic hunger.

Isabel broke his thoughts with her traditional sing-song voice for the end of a conversation. Once he'd hung up he gave his full attention to Veronica.

She was now sitting on the edge of the leather wing-back chair. She looked as if she would literally jump out of her skin. She was shaking and averting her gaze from him. He wanted to close the space between them and calm her; however, he was the cause of her fear. He could only imagine the thoughts that were running in her head. Seeing that he wasn't very good at playing make believe his options for her thought pattern quickly ran out. He didn't get a chance to ask her what she was thinking because she slowly shifted her gaze in his direction. The look on her face froze time. Her slanted eyes had glossed over and she had paled. As haunting as her face was her voice was even more chilling.

"My mother..." She spoke.

Al just stared at the breathtaking beautiful woman sitting across the office from him. Finally, after staring at Veronica for what seemed like ages, he spoke.

"What?"

"My mother will be worried. I have her car and I am to pick her up from work in a few minutes." She stared at Al as if seeing him for the first time. "May I use your phone?" The request showed a hint of emotion from Veronica. Al was happy to see it; for a moment, he was certain that she was in shock.

"Certainly" He made a motion with his hand that reminded Veronica of an usher at the theater when showing a patron to their seat. Veronica was leery of getting too close to the captivating man opposite her. She made her way to the desk intentionally maneuvering around to the side that Al was not standing on.

Al made no motion to give Veronica any space to get to the phone that he was standing by. With shaky hands Veronica picked up the phone and began punching in the numbers. About half way through dialing the number she gave Al a look that pleaded for a little space. *Don't beg, begging is not becoming of you.* He thought to himself and let the small step he took closer to her show he had no intentions of granting her plea.

She finished dialing the number and waited for her mother to answer her line.

"Hey Ma, Are you almost ready?" Veronica asked trying to sound her usual self.

"Yeah baby, but why are you still at the CaSa office?" Tammy inquired after seeing the number listed on the caller I.D. at her job. Veronica had completely forgotten her mother would have privy to her location.

"Well that's why I'm calling. It's run over and I need you to come get your car and I'll just take the train home. Is that okay?" Veronica asked Tammy hoping her mother would fall for the ploy.

"Yeah I guess so. I'll take the loop over and pick it up. Where is it parked?"

"In the pit." Veronica winced as soon as she disclosed the location of her mother's car. The "pit" was the cheapest parking in the downtown area. It was cheap for a reason. It's located all the way down by the lake and not near anything but the football stadium. It was at the bottom of a hill and the owners rarely plowed the drive making it impossible for patrons to safely navigate to a parking slot. Nonetheless, it was a popular lot, it was cheap, and it had begun to get a reputation, good and not so good. Once Veronica had given her mother the slot number that her car could be found in, she wished her goodnight and promised to call her once she got home.

Upon hanging up Veronica had gained most of her composure back and was not going to let Al Carter impose his will on her a moment longer. She snapped her head up to meet his penetrating stare and gave him a lethal look. Then simply said "Move" to him and made a point to try to push past his impressive frame. *That's what I like. Make me work for it. Put up the fight!* Something about Veronica's demeanor had him hooked. She wasn't confrontational, but she had a fighting spirit that she used to the best of her ability.

"No." Al didn't shout, or even get nasty with his response, he just simply wouldn't move out of her way. "You came around the desk the other way. I think that you should return that way." Raising an eyebrow and crossing his arms over his chest, he was deliberately challenging her. Not to be backed down, Veronica did something she had never done in her life, she grabbed Al by the back of his neck and pulled him to her and kissed him. Not just a peck or even a tender exchange. This kiss was demanding, motivated, and pure lust inspired.

Al returned her invitation and gave more than she had expected. She had only kissed him to break his stance but her plan backfired and now he had become the aggressor. She couldn't control herself. Moisture began to seep into her underwear and she stiffened at the revelation. Al felt her body go rigid but had no thoughts of stopping, this time he was going to make her his. *What am I thinking, make her mine? I can't take her here, can I? If I stop there won't be a next time. I...* Veronica's moan invaded his personal war and made the decision for him.

The next thing they both knew he had her bent over his desk and was slowly stroking her womanhood through the covering of her moist panties. He was enjoying the view of all that he could see. Her hair was wild, her lipstick had been long ago kissed off and now what remained were natural rose-colored soft lips, and she was in an "assume the position" type stance over his desk. When he had had enough of making her purr by touching her, he sat in his chair and replaced his hand and fingers with his mouth. Veronica let out what could only be described as a wail. Her knees buckled and Al was quick to grab her and place her on all four on his desk.

He continued his oral assault on her licking and lapping at all she had to offer. Veronica had no clue as to when her panties had been removed; in fact she had no inkling as to how or when her shirt and skirt no longer occupied her body. Al spent several minutes admiring Veronica's pink, pulsating cavern before he made his way to other parts of her succulent body. He traced a path with his tongue around the spherical flesh of her buttocks, causing her to flinch when he made his way in between the two of them. She reached at nothing in particular when he buried his face in her. Feeling like she had to say something she made an attempt to vocalize her pleasure but all that came out was "oooh, aaah, ah, ah, ah, shit! Yeah! Oooo!"

With fluid motion Al laid Veronica on her back and continued his oral exploration starting with her luscious mouth. Leaving the comfort of her sweet lips he made his way down her neck with fluttering kisses then switching to hard suckling on the damp skin between her ample breasts. Stopping to partake of each round chocolate mound, his warm mouth made Veronica quiver uncontrollably and arch her back in a greedy motion for him to take more. If she didn't know any better she would have sworn that things like this only happened in a book or the movies.

That's it, that's it. Yeah give in, give in to it. Look at her, she's beautiful. His thoughts were on overload; his nostrils were on red alert filled with her scent. The perfume mixed with her natural aroma was intoxicating. She arched her back off the mahogany desk and succumbed to the passion that was boiling in her. The sweat beading on her forehead was nothing more than a potent aphrodisiac for him. He couldn't take her unintended seduction any longer. With unlabored strength he picked her supple frame up and positioned her atop him in his chair. Veronica's eyes flew open at the realization that he had disrobed himself. He saw the sudden reservation plastered on her face. She made an attempt at speaking but nothing came out. Trying again she regained her voice.

"Al...I...um." She really wasn't sure what to say.

"Tell me, what's my name short for?" He wanted her to know him. He had an unearthly need for Veronica Parker to know him, mind, soul, and body. Not only did he want her to know him, he wanted to know her, he wanted her. At that moment he knew that she was to be his, she was to be his mate in life.

"What?" Confusion clearly etched on her face.

"Al. It's obviously short for something, what is it?" The passion burning in his eyes stilled her. Biting her lip Veronica shrugged her shoulders; she didn't know what Al was short for. "I don't know what it's short for."

"Alas, it seems that you don't know everything about CaSa," he said just before he placed a small kiss near her ear.

"I never said I did. So are you going to tell me?" She broke their embrace to look into his eyes.

"My name is Alejandro." He stated matter-of-factly.

"Oh, you're Spanish?"

"No, not exactly." He answered with a smile. "My mother is from Brazil"

"Oh."

The innocence of the whole exchange and Veronica herself brought Al back to fever pitch within seconds and his large member grew to an incredible size. Cupping her bottom he guided her onto his manhood with a powerful thrust. Almost instantly he noticed the unshed tears in her eyes and the extreme tightness of her vaginal walls. *Oh my god! She can't be, she is! What the hell, she's a goddamn virgin!* He was totally unprepared for this type of revelation at that particular time. It was too late to stop. They had made intimate contact and there was no turning around. With concern for her comfort he picked her up and carried her to the leather sofa that they'd shared earlier. After laying her on her back he reentered her, this time much more slowly and gently.

Veronica moaned her approval and dug her nails into his back. The pain of it all was surpassed by the pleasure being experienced by both. Al stayed his position and gave Veronica all the time she needed to accommodate his large engorged sexual organ. He took cue from her, once she began to move her hips he began to rotate his own. Her breathless surrender caused her to buck against his groin and bite his earlobe to stifle her screams.

Veronica was exhausted but she didn't care. She was afraid he might stop his assault on her senses if he knew that she was worn. Suspecting that she might be suffering some discomfort in her back from having her legs in such a position, Al scooped Veronica up and placed her on top of him. Sliding down to get optimum penetration, He slid himself inside her. Suckling her breast Al brought Veronica to a sexual zenith many times before he thought about giving in to his own release. Sensing his own plateau crowning, Al asked Veronica to open her eyes.

"Say my name Veronica." He instructed in a thick course voice.

"A…Al" She breathlessly whispered.

"No, my full name Veronica!" He ordered.

"Alejandro, oh Alejandro" she yelled.

"That's it baby, say it again."

"Alejandro, Alejandro." She whispered by his ear. The way his name rolled off her tongue made him suspect that she spoke Spanish, probably fluently. She'd just called his name and spoken to his soul. He wanted to be that for her; her soul, her protector, her all.

"Yes baby, say it again please" he pleaded close to her ear as his grasp on her tightened. She complied and yelled his given name over and over until they both climaxed together, her in sobs of pleasure and his in one long primal growl.

Chapter Six

The drive back from Detroit was pleasant for the two women. Renee had suggested that they go to celebrate Veronica's new employment. Although that was an underlying reason, Renee could sense that Veronica needed some rest and relaxation. There had been a time in both of their lives when the world seemed so small and their problems so big and gargantuan.

Renee sat in the passenger seat of the rental car staring out the window lost in thoughts of the past. Her thoughts had lingered on the day that she and Veronica went to the waterfront park together the first time. It was late April and the girls had been planning to go to Edgewater Park all month. Renee couldn't believe how excited Veronica was about it all. Everyday Veronica would talk about how she was going to wake up early that Saturday morning and call her best friend and go to the "beach".

Renee had been quite annoyed with Veronica's excitement. She didn't understand at the time why Veronica was so excited to go to the beach; it wasn't like they lived near the ocean. They were going to a local park on Lake Erie; in addition to that it was April so it was still chilly out. Renee's enlightenment came when they'd arrived at Edgewater bright and early on the day planned. It wasn't particularly nice outside that day; in fact the weather had been dreadful. It was raining out, the sand looked dirty, and they were the only ones there. Veronica made a point of having Renee spend the night at her home just so they could ride their bikes together.

Renee wanted to have one of their parent's drive them there because she wasn't particular about pedaling her bike for two plus miles, but Veronica wouldn't hear of it. Upon arrival Renee was ready to leave, truth be told she didn't want to go in the first place, but her friend's happiness took precedence over her salty disposition.

Once there Veronica played in the puddles like she was a toddler. She ran into the water with rolled up pants. And when it began to rain again, she stood at the waters edge with her arms outstretched and her head tilted back to let the rain splash her face. One would have thought that Veronica had never seen the waterfront, or been in the rain for that matter. Renee, however, just saw Veronica for what she was. She showed that no matter what was going on around her, no matter how adverse a situation could seem, some dirty sand and murky water, could bring joy and peace to her problems.

Veronica, that day, shared a portion of herself that at the time she was only privy to. She looked at life through a romantic lens. Many people could and would classify Veronica as a workaholic, serious even. Not Renee. To Renee, Veronica would always be as beautiful inside as the moment they shared on a cold April morning many years before.

"He thinks that I'm a virgin Renee." Renee's head snapped to attention at her friend's disclosure.

"What do you mean?" Renee interrogated.

"I mean he said that I should have told him that I had not been 'de-flowered.'" Veronica removed her hands off the steering wheel to make quotation mark symbols with her fingers and then quickly replaced them on the wheel.

Renee tried to muffle her giggles as she said "Oh girl, he did not say deflowered did he?" She was near hysterics at the mere thought of him saying something as honorable as "deflowering."

"I'm pleased that you find this all so amusing. You know we haven't talked since then." Veronica hadn't wanted to tell her friend that she and Al had not spoken in more than a week.

"Why not?" Renee asked skeptically.

"Because he hasn't called." Veronica answered half-heartedly. If truth had been told, Veronica had utilized her caller I.D. to its fullest. Any call that remotely looked as if it were originating from Al Carter she didn't answer. Renee could tell that her friend was only telling a portion of the truth if she was telling the truth at all.

"Ronnie, cut the bull okay. How did you find out that you had got the job then?"

"Simon Jr. his brother, he called about two days after the interview and told me that if I wanted the job it was mine. He said I was his favorite and he was so proud of me and all this other stuff." Veronica was trying to downplay the situation. Veronica was very modest about her accomplishments; it was one of her traits that Renee enjoyed most about her.

They rode in silence for another forty-five minutes until they reached their exit to get off the turnpike and onto the interstate that would take them directly into Cleveland. Once the toll had been paid Renee decided to broach the subject again. If there were a thing about Veronica that could completely annoy the living hell out of Renee; her inopportune moments of silence would definitely be the winner.

"So, what's going to happen when you start the job?" Not giving Veronica a chance to answer, Renee continued. "I mean you can't very well avoid each other, and it's obvious that you like him."

Veronica swerved the car and almost ran into an SUV full of wide-eyed seniors. Once she gained her composure she offered her apologies to her fellow motorist. "How dare you imply that I even remotely think of him as more than my boss?" She asked almost too calmly. The peace in her voice was not lost on her friend. However, Renee decided to keep that comment to herself.

"And how dare you try to fool me, your best friend, that you, don't care about him." Renee shot back a little too vehemently for Veronica's taste.

"What's with you anyway? And just so you know I haven't changed over night and I most certainly do not and will not 'care about' some man that I hardly know and had one night of foolishness with. Now, if you don't mind I would like to drop the subject." Veronica had hoped that would be the end of the conversation but knew better and braced her self for what she knew to be lethal, Renee's tongue.

"Oh hell naw!" Renee's outburst let Veronica know that the real conversation had just begun. In fact there was not going to be a conversation. There was going to be plenty of talking but it would be only one of them doing it. "First of all." All of Renee's tirades began with "First of all". "I don't know who the hell you think you are but I know who I am and who I am is Renee Charleston best friend to and all knowing of Veronica Parker the most sensitive, caring, self confident, intelligent, person I know. Now far be it for me to pass judgment on anyone," she gave Veronica a "Don't go there" look before she interrupted. "Since we both know I give everybody a fair shake, you must know that I've given you about all the shakes that you're allowed. I think, no, scratch that, I know that you like him. As a matter of fact let me go on record and say that it's more than just like! You have never opened up to any man outside of Nick and this...this stranger waltzes in and boom! You're creaming your goddamn panties! So wake up sweetie, you are fallin' and if you ain't careful it's gonna hurt!" Renee hadn't realized that she was screaming until she noticed that Veronica's eyes were watery. Renee looked out the window and noticed for the first time since she had begun her soliloquy that the car was no longer moving and they were now in the parking lot of a Denny's. Veronica tried to blink back her unshed tears to no avail and soon one trickled down her cheek, then another, and another. Between her cries she looked at her friend. She wanted Renee to understand everything that was tearing her apart on the inside. She needed someone to understand the turmoil she was in.

Cleaning her face she managed to say to Renee "It already hurts." Then she began to wail and sob in Renee's arms.

****

"Well this is the most I've seen you in your office in weeks, what's the occasion?" Isabel was standing in her employer's office doorway. Al had been incognito for almost two weeks opting to be more hands on at the restaurant site. The finishing touches had been made to the offices there and he decided that his best option would be to work there. More importantly, he decided to move his office location to the site because he was beyond distracted sitting in his office at the office building. Every time he walked into the room he was reminded of Veronica. Her hair, her eyes, her sweet luscious mouth, her whimpers and moans of pure ecstasy, she was branded to his memory.

What made matters worse was the apparent fact that she did not want to be bothered with him. He had called and even sent her an e-mail, only to have her send response to him via Isabel or to only communicate with his brother. He was sure that Isabel knew that something had transpired between him and Veronica; she was just merciful enough not to mention it to him.

Veronica was to start her position the next day. It had been three weeks since he'd made love to her in his office and he had not been right ever since. The circumstance of her seemingly being a virgin nagged him to the point that he was loosing sleep over it. She, in his eyes, deserved to be loved for the first time not on his desk or love seat in his office, but in bed, by a man that could give her everything. Sure he had monetary wealth, but he was not so certain that he could provide her with what she needed emotionally. The thought had provoked another restless night for him. Was he really considering being more to Veronica than just a colleague? Could he be seriously inviting the thought of performing the act of love with her again? Hell yes!

Veronica had attacked his senses with a simple look, a minor brushing of lips, and a lingering memory of her smile. He'd come so undone with her that he found himself in a cold shower the night before last trying to subdue his hunger for her. However, this thinking about Veronica had him so upset that it was beginning to interfere with his work.

A week prior, while sitting in a meeting with the representative from the art dealership, he jumped to his feet when he saw her walk past the conference room with his father. The other four persons in the room thought something was wrong and Al covered himself saying that he was going to try to catch his father and see if he would like to give an opinion on the pieces they all had selected. By the time he properly excused himself his father and Veronica were gone.

"Bel, I've actually missed you this past week. Don't spoil it with your sarcasm." He said rising to his feet. Al was known to show up at the office much earlier than most and leave later than all, except Isabel. He knew that she was somewhere in the building when he arrived that mourning around 7:30. He figured she was out distributing rental receipts. It was the beginning of the second week in December and the tenants paid for office space on a bi-annual basis.

"I won't spoil anything, that's more in your department." She said with an all-knowing grin on her face.

"Yes, well, I suppose if you say so." He wanted to say more but couldn't. What had happened between Veronica and he happened three weeks prior and those three weeks had been the most excruciatingly painful ordeal he'd ever experienced in life. He didn't relay the events of that day to any one, so his pain was magnified by his self-inflicted seclusion.

Al had been at the office for approximately ninety minutes and this was his first time seeing anyone that day. He was eager to run from there, but he couldn't justify being at the site another day. The flooring had been completed a week ahead of schedule, and the management team had been hired and were to start within the week. Along with Veronica, the General Manager, Executive Chef and his staff, two Assistant Manager's, and two other Sales Managers were to get acquainted with each other and the CaSa staff the next day at breakfast and then begin acclimating them selves to their new roles at Four Corners.

Four Corners took up the entire 57th, 58th and 59th floors of the tallest building in the city. It had taken CaSa more than four years to negotiate the rental of space with the owners and another two of convincing city hall to change the zoning and give them the go ahead.

Al had to admit that he'd done a very good job of developing this particular project. His father and brother both thought that it was too big a project for him. In Al's mind his family, with the exception of his mother, always made improper assumptions about him. Al received more evidence for this conclusion the prior Sunday. Sunday's in the Carter family was a day to join together and relax, play catch up, and occasionally entertain a few guests who were considered close friends.

This Sunday Samantha had invited herself over to his parent's house so that she could force herself into Al's personal space and time. Since his interlude with Veronica he'd made no attempt at continuing his and Samantha's casual relationship.

Samantha called Al the night before to tell, not ask, but tell him that she would be accompanying him to church with his family and staying for dinner. She'd said that she and his mother had run into each other at a boutique and thought that it would be lovely if Samantha joined them. While Al had no doubt that his mother was just being friendly and extending an invitation to a woman that she'd known her son to be involved with, he did suspect that Samantha's motive was less than honorable.

By the time the Carter's reached their sprawling home located in an affluent east side suburb Al was more than ready to be rid of Samantha Riley. She had affected this syrupy sweet voice and was clinging to him as if they were joined at the hip. After Church Al let Samantha know that he wasn't impressed with her façade.

"What's the matter sweetheart, I thought that we were having a good time." Samantha said innocently.

"Cut the Crap! Why are you acting like this? And what's this 'sweetheart' stuff anyway?" Al was livid.

"Listen Al, I'm just in a good mood today. I can't help it if you're a sourpuss. I think I should be the one asking you what the deal is." She stated defensively. She crossed her slender arms over what he seemingly noticed for the first time, small chest. He noted that Veronica's was fuller and more satisfying than the woman sitting in the passenger seat of his sedan.

Shaking away thoughts of Veronica he brought his mind back to Samantha and her strange behavior. He made an effort to smooth the situation over before it turned into an argument. "I'm sorry. I guess I'm just tired and a little cranky, sorry." Al placed his hand on her knee in a soothing gesture. Out the corner of his eye he could see the victorious look that Samantha was trying to conceal.

At that moment he knew there was more to her behavior than what she was letting on.

It didn't take much longer to validate Al's reservations about his companion for the day. Once Al's sister-in-law Janet put his twin niece and nephew down for a nap, everyone went to the large family room to watch television and talk. Sitting in his favorite armchair, Simon Carter Sr. summoned his wife to his side. Mariana Sa-Carter was a stunning beauty in her youth, age only added to her profound looks.

It was love at first sight for Simon Carter when he saw his wife to be walking along the beach. He and his father were vacationing in Brazil. It was a graduation present to Simon for completing his undergraduate courses with honors. While there they had taken tours of Sao Paolo and Rio de Janeiro and were to go to Belo Horizante in two days.

He was walking along Copa Cabana beach taking in the splendid sights of people laying in the sun and gorgeous women sauntering along in their bikinis when he looked and saw her. There Mariana sat on a yellow towel in a red two piece swim set. Her hair was flowing with the cool breeze off the ocean, she was perfect, tall, slender yet curvy, and beautiful. That day Simon was carrying his camera and he decided that he had to have a picture of her because he probably would never see her again. Turned out she was on his and his father's flight from Rio to Belo. Born and Raised in Belo, Mariana was taking a sabbatical from her collegiate studies and was returning home to finish school.

Simon Sr. smiled as he reminisced to the day he first saw his wife. It never ceased to amaze him that the only picture that came out clear on that roll was the one he took of Mariana. The picture had been enlarged and now hung above the mantel in the Carter's family room.

Once Mariana sat on the armrest of her husband's chair she placed a kiss atop his head. Al sat on the over-stuffed loveseat next to Samantha while his brother and sister-in-law were enthralled in an intense game of chess at the game table. The whole scene could warm hearts, but not Al's. He was completely turned off by something that he couldn't quite put his finger on. Then like a deer caught in headlights he realized that he was in a trap.

Mariana spoke first. "So when Sam called me and said she wanted to go shopping I was completely surprised! I could not believe it when she told me that you two were so serious about each other." Al grimaced at his mother's attempt at casual conversation. He, along with the rest of the Carter clan, knew that Samantha was not his mother's favorite person. Her distaste for the younger woman was even more apparent when her accent became more pronounced. Her Brazilian accent always became thicker when she was upset.

Al decided not blow up at Samantha once he discovered she'd lied to him about the meeting between his mother and her. He wanted to see how far Sam had and would take the scene. He didn't have to wait long for his father spoke next. "So Son, your mother tells me that you've been keeping secrets from us?" Simon Jr. and Janet had stopped playing chess and joined the rest of the people in the room. Standing next to his wife Simon Jr. entered the conversation and asked, "So when's the big day, and don't tell me that you two plan to elope, I don't think mom could handle any more surprises." Al truly adored his brother and thought the world of his petite soft-spoken wife, but at that moment he would have liked nothing better than to jump out of his seat and strangle his older sibling.

Turning to Samantha, he downed the rest of his brandy before he spoke. "So what secrets are we keeping from everyone sweetheart?" purposely dragging out the last word.

"Well" Samantha said trying to buy herself time "I was telling your mother yesterday how you and I were discussing marriage and children and how we were going to one day fulfill those dreams." Al was so amused by it all, everyone with the exception of his mother was pleased to believe that Al had finally made the right choice and was going to settle down with Sam. Al straightened from his hunched over position and placed his empty glass on the marble end table. "Well Dad, what do you think about all of this?" Al had come to the realization that he'll always be fragile in the eyes of his Father. However, accepting that view of him didn't take the hurt of it away.

His father told him that he thought it was wonderful that he'd decided to choose such an independent and headstrong woman as his companion. The rest of the evening went by in a blur for Al. Two more glasses of brandy found him sleeping off the effects in a guestroom in his parent's home. Al hadn't called Samantha and she had not called him, but needless to say it became very apparent when he refused to say goodbye to her when Simon Jr. gave her a ride home that they would no longer be seeing each other.

Chapter Seven

It had been more than three weeks since Veronica had last seen Al; it felt more like three years. Along with the rest of the management team, she got a chance to take her first formal tour of the restaurant facilities and get aquatinted with the layout. The General Manager was a gentleman named George who, like Nick, was very proud of his Greek heritage. She liked him. He wasn't pushy, or too overbearing, nor did he try to force himself on anyone in the room. In her experience, Veronica had come across many executives and businessmen alike and, most of them seemed as if they had to let you know they were in charge. She detested that sort of attitude in men. Maybe because it seemed to come so naturally for them to do so.

Veronica's former boss at the hotel she worked for was that way. If someone began to show fear or reverence of him when he walked into a room, his eyes would light up. There were many words she'd used to describe her feelings for such people; most times they began with the letter R, repulsive, repugnant, and ridiculous. George was laid back in an authoritative way. He didn't divert the conversation to his accomplishments when someone was speaking of his or hers', he did however make it clear that he expected those same results and more.

Chef Brasilio was a complete character, he like Al, was half-Brazilian. But unlike Al he claimed a French parent. He spoke to everyone and even came onto Isabel who, to Veronica's surprise, blushed at his advance. The staff breakfast was going very well, they had all agreed on the final menu tasting dates and had even agreed to push back the opening date by one week so that Four Corners would make it's premier on Valentines day.

Veronica was in the middle of a conversation with one of the Sales team manager's when a sudden chill ran down her spine. Al walked into the room. *Damn! I didn't have to turn around to know he came in the goddamn room! This is so not fair!* Not to alarm her co-worker, Veronica tried to maintain her train of thought and complete the conversation about possible grand opening promotions.

When Al walked into the conference room he was aware that there were other occupants present, but he only saw Veronica. She had her hair pinned up into a bun at the back of her head. Al liked the more refined look on her, it made her eyes appear more slanted and elongated her neck. She wore a simple wine colored button-up shirt and wide legged black pants that were accented with cuffs, and closed toe pumps that were the same color as her shirt. Again the only make-up she wore was lipstick, this time the color was a deep wine almost the shade of her shirt. Al thought her lips looked as if the coloring came from sweet ripe cherries.

Veronica felt this moment was as good as any to finally speak to Al it had, after all, been three weeks since they last spoke. She finished her conversation with her fellow worker and politely excused herself. Making her way slowly across the room she couldn't keep the thoughts away of his powerful yet gentle hands exploring her aching body. *Damn he looks good. I can't believe this! Do I look okay? What the hell am I gonna do, I can't keep on like this.* She placed her rampant thoughts at bay and made a move to get Al's attention. She was going to touch his arm so that he could turn around but he spun in her direction before she could move her hand.

"You don't have to look so startled Veronica, I am fully aware of you." The statement spoke volumes. How did he link into her so well? It was as if the day in his office was happening all over again. Except this time they weren't touching, but it was just as intense. Veronica half expected him to be as connected to her as she was to him, but in her limited experience with men she'd grown to think that they weren't as perceptive as women.

"I am a little startled." She said, "What did you think? That I wouldn't be freaked out, it's like you, well you...I don't know but you knew I was near. That scares me." Veronica was taken back at how soft her voice was, a barely audible whisper. Veronica felt uncomfortable and her body language proved to Al that she was. Her arms were crossed and she was in a hostile pose.

"You don't have to be afraid of me." Over the three-week period Al let his goatee grow in. It gave him a darker look, more mature, more attractive. To be honest with her self, Veronica, at that very moment, wanted to take her fingers and rub the short dark hairs that framed his full lips and strong chin.

"I'm not afraid of you. I wouldn't have accepted the position if I were." Al noted the confrontational tone of Veronica's voice. No matter how adverse a subject matter or situation she had a way of not letting her opposition see her sweat. Something about the woman that stood before him made Al want to leap out his skin. She was intelligent, combative, alluring, and unknowingly seductive.

"Veronica we are going to have to be on polite maybe even friendly terms with one another, so why not try to start now?" Veronica was thankful that he hadn't brought up the day in his office again, not that she'd expected him to, but she was a quick study and learned to expect the unex-pected when it came to Al Carter.

Not to be outdone in the department of civility Ve-ronica made her opinion known on the subject. "I agree, Mr. Carter." She'd intentionally used his formal name to get under his skin and looking at his cold expression, the tactic had been a success. *Note to self: He does not like me calling him Mr. Carter. Guess I'll have to do that more often.* As if reading her mind Al spoke in an almost lethal tone. "I trust that you understand every word that is coming from my mouth. You have two choices, address me as Al or Alejan-dro, either one will be fine. But if you address me as Mr.

Carter again I'll personally make sure that you never do it again."

Al made as if he were going to move and let the conversation end that way, but Veronica was not about to back down. She sidestepped into his path. Although he stood several inches above her, Veronica was determined not to let him pass. "Do not ever and I mean ever, try to use intimidation and idle threats on me again. You may be my employer and yes we may even have to work closely together on some choice projects, but I am not your average girl, so don't mistake me for one, Mr. Carter." It was now her turn to move past him but before she could move Al leaned down to better angle himself to look her in the eyes. The fire that was raging in him could take out a forest but Veronica stayed her ground and reciprocated his heated stare.

"I warned you Veronica, now you will deal with the consequences." The contrast of the calm of his voice to the rage exhibited on his face was amazing. She wasn't sure which he was forcing himself to restrain. Al straightened himself and almost as quickly as his rage appeared, it dissipated. Without another word he glided past her. It must have been a few minutes before she made her way back over to the group of people who were exploding with laughter at something Chef Brasilio said.

****

"So how was your first day?" Tammy asked her daughter. They had agreed to have dinner together at Tammy's near east side home. Tammy preferred it to living on the east side. Tammy spent her childhood and most of her adult life on the east side of Cleveland and she was looking for a change. Albeit not a dramatic change like moving to California, but it was a change nonetheless.

"It was what it was, just a way for us all to get acquainted and lay out our plans and goals." Veronica pushed the food around on her plate like rocks in a sand garden.

Tammy was becoming impatient with her only child and told her so. "What's the matter with you? You come in here moping and all. I won't have it. What is it, uh?" For the first time since they sat down to eat Veronica looked up from her food. The anguish in her eyes alerted Tammy to what she suspected to be true. Something was amiss with her daughter and she had every intention to find out what it was.

"I'm waiting." Tammy said before she placed a forkful of candied yams in her mouth, never taking her eyes off her daughter.

"I don't want to talk about it Ma." Veronica held a glimmer of hope that she could pacify her mother's inquisition but knew that she could not.

"I truly and honestly don't give a damn what you don't want to talk about." Tammy had placed her fork and knife down, leaned back into her chair, and gave Veronica a 'don't mess with me' look.

"I lied to you the day of the interview." Veronica blurted out. She'd only intended to tell her mother enough to calm her curiosity but before she could stop her self she was telling her mother how she'd placed her job and career in jeopardy. Tammy took in all that Veronica told her. She sensed that her daughter was holding something back and asked her if she was. Veronica shook her head in response.

"What is it?"

"I had sex with him the day of the interview, in his office." There was nothing but silence for what seemed like forever. The loud silent air was finally broken into when Tammy let out a long audible sigh.

"Wha...Wha...I...Damn!" Tammy was dumbfounded. She couldn't believe what she had heard come from the mouth of her child.

"Ma, say something." Veronica pleaded with her mother.

"I really don't have much to say, you slept with him and now he's got you all messed up in the head. Actually, it's really funny." Tammy started laughing and Veronica couldn't believe what was transpiring. She'd told her mother that she had sex with her employer and that she feared that it may tarnish her image and ruin her career, and her mother had the nerve to think that it was somehow humorous.

The look of disbelief on Veronica's face quieted Tammy some but she still had to stifle her laughter.

"Girl don't you worry about your job, that will be there. Remember CaSa only owns part of the restaurant, yes they will be responsible for operations but nothing you did was illegal." Tammy was a Paralegal for a large firm in the city and she had gone over all of the contracts and hand-books just to be sure Veronica had not missed anything pertinent.

"What you need to be concerned about is when you'll tell him that you love him." Tammy stated matter-of-factly. Veronica's attention was yanked back to reality.

What?" she yelled at her mother. Shaking her head wildly, Veronica tried to clear her head. "Have you really lost it? Were you drinking or something before I got here? Nick said that he always wonders if you're all there, now, I tend to agree with him."

"Veronica, don't be so goddamn dramatic. It's not even that serious. I may have had you at a young age but I know that you never gave any man the time of day. Wake up girl something about this brother has got you hooked. And if I may say so myself, it's about damn time."

"He's not black you know." It was the only response Veronica could think of. Her mother just told her that she was in love with a man, her boss, and there was nothing that she could do about it.

"I know he's not black, child. 'Brother' is just a term. Besides, you are a beautiful and intelligent young woman. You have the right to be attracted to whom ever you want, regardless of race." Veronica was completely shocked at her mother's nonchalant attitude. Tammy continued, "Does he know about your past?"

"What past, Ma?" Veronica had never revealed the circumstances of her lost virginity to her mother so she was apprehensive to find out exactly what her mother was referring to.

"The abortion, Ronnie."

"How do you know about that?" Other than Renee and Nick, Veronica had not told anyone of the secret she held for almost ten years.

"I picked up the phone one night when you and Renee were having one of your all night gab fests and I listened. It was right after I had come back into town from the Mock Trial competition in Columbus, remember?" Veronica had remembered all to well. She was fifteen and scared. There was a boy named Justin that she'd met while with a friend at a suburban mall. Justin was five years older than she was. The age difference didn't matter to her or her mother. Veronica had brought him home to meet her mother about a month after they started dating.

Things were going good for them, they went out to few movies together and he would meet her at the library so she could tutor him for his GED test. Justin was a high school drop out. He idolized his older brother Marc who was attending a local junior college and Justin told her that he'd aspired to be just like his big brother.

One day Veronica and Justin made a date to go to his and his brother's home and watch some movies he'd rented. Veronica, Justin, and Marc were all sitting on the sofa watching a poorly made action film. Marc left the room to give Veronica and his brother some privacy, or at least that was the excuse he'd used. Shortly after he vacated the room, Veronica and Justin began kissing and soon they no longer cared what was on the television.

Veronica wanted to have sex with Justin. She did not have the same desire to sleep with his brother. Once She and Justin had moved from the living room to his room, they had intercourse. She was a willing partner. Justin rose off the bed and told Veronica not to move and that he'd be right back. Veronica lay in the dark for a few minutes before the door reopened and in walked Marc. She scrambled to pull the bed sheets over her exposed flesh.

"Ronnie don't cover up. I just wanna talk to you."

"O...k...kay." She quivered out.

"Listen, you know we all family, right?" She was silent so he continued. "Well you know what's in the family is shared by family, so I think that you should be more than willing to show me the love you gave my brother."

"I don't know about that, Marc. I don't think that's such a good idea." Veronica had just given her most precious gift to someone that she believed she loved and he in turn had set her up! "Where's your brother?" She asked rising off the bed but Marc firmly pushed her back.

Although he hadn't gotten physical with her, Veronica was scared. She was so afraid that Marc would take what he wanted from her and she couldn't bare the thought. Marc took off his clothing and without preamble, mounted Veronica's quaking body. Marc, unlike his brother, didn't bother with any formalities before he entered her body. Veronica began to cry and Marc told her to shut up because it was what she wanted.

Veronica left Justin and Marc's house while they slept and hadn't seen either since. About six weeks later Veronica found herself at the free clinic with an STD and pregnant. She was too ashamed to turn to her mother for help so her only option was to turn to Nick. Nick never asked her what happened or where the father of the child was. He'd told Tammy that he'd take care of Veronica while she was out of town at the competition.

When Tammy left town a month after Veronica discovered she was with child, Nick took her to the clinic and Veronica's life was changed forevermore.

Veronica looked at her mother as if seeing her for the first time in her life. "If you knew all this time, why didn't you say something?" Veronica couldn't fathom a reason to explain her mother's silence.

"Because you'd suffered enough, Ronnie. And I was hurting for you baby. I can't be any help to you if at the time I felt like I was no help. You felt as if you couldn't turn to me, Ronnie. I was hurt. I'm so sorry baby." Tammy shed one solitary tear. Veronica watched as the droplet slid down her mother's cheek, she was entranced by it. In her life Veronica couldn't remember Tammy ever crying. She'd seen her mother's eyes look as if she were about to cry but not shed a tear. Tammy changed before her daughter's eyes. Veronica saw her mother in a new light; she was someone that had fallacies and visible faults. Tammy Parker was a person with feelings, feelings that Veronica had taken for granted.

"Ma, I'm the one who's sorry. I didn't come to you because I didn't think that I could handle your disappointment in me." Veronica confessed.

"You never have to worry about me and my feelings towards you. You are my heart and soul." Tammy's voice had begun to shake and she was now unabashedly letting her long held tears flow. "When I heard the conversation between you and Renee I couldn't believe what I was hearing." Veronica tried to interrupt but Tammy put up her hand to silence her child. "I hurt so much for you. You didn't ask for that, you damn sure didn't deserve it. I wanted to go out and find those jackasses who hurt you and make them pay for what they did." Tammy paused to wipe her tears with a napkin.

"I wanted to be there for you, but I knew that with me going to school and all you felt as if I were to busy for you." She paused to gather her thoughts and continued, because Tammy had waited nearly ten years to say these things to her daughter. She'd tried to figure out the best-case scenario in which to broach the subject, but could never find one. Eventually days, turned into months, which lead to years, too many years.

"I needed you to understand that you could talk to me, but you never did. I thought you'd healed but you seemed to get worse. Not talking to boys, never bringing any home, you even closed yourself off from girls. I felt helpless. Instead of stepping forward to help, I backed off and tried to let you handle it. I was wrong. I did you more harm than good."

Veronica sat with her mother for another hour talking, reminiscing, and healing. They discussed many things including the fact that Veronica had a clouded past and Tammy felt that she needed to share this information with Al before they went any further in a relationship. Veronica kindly reminded her mother that there was no relationship, and just because she'd shared an intimate moment with him, he had no rights to any aspects of her personal life.

Chapter Eight

Veronica's life altered dramatically in the week following the revelation that her mother knew about her secret. Since that day, it seemed as if her eyes were opened to many new facets about Tammy. She'd found out that Tammy and Nick were once involved and stopped seeing each other because Nick called it quits. Since her and her mother's conversation Veronica had even entertained the thought of being more than civil to Al. Although it only lasted a short period, she'd at least had the thought.

Walking into her office the following Monday after the staff breakfast meeting and her heated encounter with Al, Veronica switched on the light to find a white package with a red bow sitting on her desk. Veronica stared at the box for at least five minutes before moving closer to it. She was sure that it was for her and she was more than positive whom it was from. She was afraid to touch it, so she didn't. Veronica managed to ignore the box for another three hours as she began compiling and updating her opening night guest list. Since there was only her and a few of the other staff on hand she was fortunate enough to not have to tell anyone about the gift box. The only other people at the restaurant were the contractors who were busy installing the modern bathroom stalls and the neon lighting in the southeast corner windows.

The ringing phone made Veronica jump. She'd been so accustomed to her solitude and she hadn't been waiting on a call so she was a little unnerved by the sound. She already knew who was on the other end of the phone before picking it up. That, more than anything scared the living daylights out of her.

"Four Corners, Sales and Event Management; Veronica speaking, how may I help you?" She answered as calmly as she could muster.

"Don't be so formal, you already know that it's me." Al replied smugly.

"I know nothing of the sort Mr. Carter."

"You do know Veronica, and I'm willing to bet that you almost let your voice mail pick up the call." Al, in a short amount of time found a way to tap into Veronica's thought pattern. It annoyed and intrigued her at the same time.

"Is there something that I can do for you, Sir?" She had no intentions of playing any mind games with Al, mainly because she was certain that she'd be on the losing end of it all.

"Open the box." *Damn! Damn! Damn! Can he not know every thing about me?*

"I don't know what you're referring to Mr. Carter. Has there been a delivery for me?" Veronica figured her best option was to play dumb.

"No there hasn't and you very well do know what I'm referring to, now open the box Veronica." Veronica took in a long breath before she picked up the box and looked at it as if were a foreign object from another planet. Slowly she removed the ribbon and wrapping paper.

Al smiled on his end of the phone as he heard the loud gasp come from Veronica.

"Al, how did you know?"

"I saw the way you lingered on that particular page when we were going through the catalogue. So consider it your opening day present." What sat before Veronica was the most beautiful desk nameplate she'd ever seen not to mention the most expensive she'd ever seen.

"Al this is completely inappropriate, I can't accept this, and it's too much."

"You can and you will. I've given each of the staff members a gift, this one just happens to be a little more special."

"I remember how much something like this cost, it must have run close to..." Al interrupted.

"Never mind how much it cost. Just accept it. Besides it got you to call me Al. That's really all I want from you, for now any way." Veronica gripped the phone tighter at Al's statement. She'd let her guard down and regretted doing so. At a lost for words she told Al a lie and said that she was backed up with work and had to finish if she wanted to get out of the office at a decent hour. Al was fully aware that she'd not told him the truth but let her go any way. He was on a business trip in New York and there wasn't much he could do to keep her on the phone hundreds of miles away.

"I'll let you go Veronica. Don't forget that we have the menu tasting Friday afternoon, so make sure to wear loose-fitting clothing. Chef Brasilio is known for making very large portions of food."

"I haven't forgotten. So long Mr. Carter." Veronica placed the receiver back in its cradle. "Well my day is completely screwed up." She said aloud to no one. Pushing away from her desk she decided that she needed to take a break from her day and get something to eat. She felt weak but for some reason she figured that it had nothing to do with lunchtime hunger. She took one last glance at the gift from her employer and decided to fully accept the gift. She removed the tissue paper from around the ebony wood and platinum rectangle desk ornament, made room for it by moving the small globe from her desk to the side book shelf and placed the nameplate where all could see its inscription, "Veronica Parker, Sales and Event Manager".

****

Friday had come way too early for Veronica's liking. She'd talked to Al everyday prior and was actually beginning to enjoy hearing his voice. Once they stayed on the line for more than an hour. During the time Al recalled how he became involved in the family business.

Veronica learned a lot about him, and it frightened her to discover that she actually enjoyed talking to him. However, what vexed her even more was that she'd become agitated one day when he didn't call her until late in the afternoon. She'd grown accustomed to hearing from him just before her lunch meal. This day though he didn't call till nearly four thirty that evening. She knew for a fact that he didn't have a meeting until after one, but he didn't bother to call until the end of her workday. It took more than her normal resilience to keep her comments at bay about his tardiness.

Veronica was the last to arrive at the tasting; she'd taken on the daunting task of the concierge program, and coordinating the Visitor's Bureau promotional luncheon. The tasting had been planned for two that afternoon as to make provision for Al's arrival back into Cleveland earlier that day. Veronica had called Isabel beforehand to notify her of possible lateness.

She was surprised to find that the rest of the staff had waited to begin until her arrival. Once there she made apology for holding up the tasting. George made a joke saying that her lateness helped them delay the potential food poisoning they were about to receive.

Veronica took her seat at one of the two tables set for the staff. Al was seated at the other table. She chanced taking a look his way only to find his gazed fixed on her face. She immediately blushed at his penetrating stare. The heat infused in her cheeks was not lost on Al. He felt as if he were spinning out of control. This woman, this beautiful voluptuous woman had taken over his mind, body, and heart. He hadn't wanted to admit that he was in love with her in such a short period of time and under such circumstances.

Al had never been in love before but by God he was sure he loved Veronica Parker.

At first he thought it was just infatuation with something so rare and exquisite, but the time they'd spent apart with only the telephone to connect them had altered him. She didn't know it, but the day he called her late was because that was the day he'd come to the vivid realization that he was in love with the woman who sat less than ten feet away.

The hard thing about loving someone was convincing him or her that they should reciprocate those feelings. He knew that he had more than just a simple task on his hands when it came to that department. Veronica wasn't an easily swayed person when it came to men. If he knew nothing else about her it was that. He noticed that she was nothing but business and almost too placid when around them.

Jumpy could be the best term to describe her when she was caught off guard or unprepared in a male's presence. At the tasting she did not disappoint. She scooted her chair away from one of the male assistant managers and her body language could only be described as defensive. The scowl on her face denoted her discomfort and Al could swear that if touched she'd leap out of her skin.

The servers brought out the appetizer sampler platters first. The restaurant theme was an eclectic mix of Cajun, South American, and Caribbean cuisine. There was an abundance of attention made to the preparation of the seafood dishes and an extra amount of time had gone into chicken and beef skewers. The most impressive dish was the large bowl of jambalaya. Each person was served a healthy portion of the spicy mixture along with cheese rolls that tasted as if they were somehow miraculously transported from an oven in Brazil.

Once the staff had been stuffed to the brim with the exotic and tantalizing food, each took his or her turn at critiquing the line up. Veronica was second to last to speak her opinion with only Al left to follow.

"Chef Brazilio you are magnificent!" She pro-
claimed, "However I would suggest that you spend a little
more time perfecting the desserts. This is a very meat and
potatoes kind of town and I fear that some of your ideas may
be a little too much for an initial opening, maybe people will
be ready for them during a menu change." Veronica got
many nods of agreement and a smile of approval from Al.
That small sign of agreement and pride from him sent a chill
through her body.

Once Al made his comments, the group made plans
to meet the following week after the Christmas Holiday.
Christmas day was less than 48 hours away and everyone
was looking forward to a little break. Veronica hadn't made
any plans to do anything. Her mother was going to Florida
to visit her Grandparents. Over the recent years Tammy
Parker had made amends with her parents and was enjoying
the time that she'd spent with them. Julius and Starla Parker
had all but disowned their youngest child when she came
home pregnant, unwed, and under the legal age to vote.

Tammy thought that she would never get over her
parents decision to send her to a maternity home. In time
though, the Parkers reconciled and Tammy saw their choice
as the best thing to ever happen to her. At the maternity
home Tammy wasn't thought of as a failure and the staff
didn't treat her as if she were diseased like her own family
did. Being at the home taught Tammy many lessons but the
most important one was that she was a person and that her
life was not worthless. She had taken everything that she
could from her time at the home and successfully instilled
those values in her daughter.

Tammy had invited her daughter to join her and the
rest of her family in the south for Christmas. Veronica was
less than enthusiastic about going to see her family and
declined her Mother's offer. Unlike her mother, Veronica
was not as forgiving to her family. For years Veronica
didn't know much less see her aunts, uncles, or grandparents
because of harbored animosity. While she was at least on

speaking terms with her family she'd yet to fully forgive all the pain and anguish they caused her mother and herself.

Veronica had decided to accept Renee's invite to have dinner with the Charleston's on Christmas Eve. She felt that was her best option seeing how she didn't want to take an extended vacation so shortly after starting in her new position.

Al, like Veronica, would be spending time with his family on Christmas Eve and had nothing planned for Christmas day. He desperately wanted to find out what her plans were for the day, for he entertained the idea of trying to convince her to come and enjoy the day with him.

While everyone was filing out of the restaurant to return to their respective offices and destinations Al lingered around and hoped that Veronica would do the same so that they may speak privately. Veronica had no such plans and made it a point to leave the room as quickly as possible without so much as a backward glance in Al's direction.

Chapter Nine

Al couldn't swallow the bitter taste left in his mouth. It was Christmas Day, he hadn't talked to Veronica, and the urge to see her had consumed him. Pacing in his apartment, Al didn't know what else to do. He'd already spoken to his entire family and wished them a joyous New Year. At the last moment the entire Carter family, with exclusion of Al, made plans to spend the holiday with the Sa's in Ouro Puerto, Brazil. Al was sorry that he was going to miss the festivities but he couldn't bring himself up to going.

Al loved Ouro Puerto. The hilly town boasted lovely museums, sidewalk cafes, cobblestone streets, and beautiful historical churches. There's this one church there that he particularly loved. It was rather gothic in style and gave Al nightmares when he was a young child, but as he grew so did his reverence for the cathedral. The church had wood planks lining the floor with numbers printed on them several spaces apart. It was when he visited the church at the age of thirteen that he'd learn that those were graves and each number coincided with the name of centuries old corpses.

Al knew that if he didn't leave the apartment soon he would go mad. With that he put on a pair of boots he had procrastinated in buying until the snow became almost unmanageable, placed a sweatshirt over his snug fitting tee shirt, and put on the rest of his winter ware. He had no set destination in mind for the only thing that occupied his thoughts was Veronica.

Although it was cold out it couldn't have been more beautiful. The snow had been falling most of the previous night and because it was a holiday there wasn't much traffic,

71

pedestrian or vehicle, to disturb the panoramic scene. Al thought about how the look of the Shaker Square area was reminiscent of the small town movie settings. It looked like a place one dreamed of when a perfect vision of Christmas day came to mind. Snow covered trees, decorations, and lights. The Christmas fare only made the already cozy and inviting setting more alluring.

He walked until his feet lead him to the entrance of Veronica's apartment building. Al hadn't realized that he'd memorized her address until one day he found himself driving past her residence hoping to catch her coming or going from it. He sat staring at the digital name scroll for what seemed like forever when an Asian couple came through the security door and with heavy accents wished him a Merry Christmas. Al caught the door before it had a chance to close completely and let himself in the building.

Before he could stop himself he was knocking on her door. She had a wreath adorning her entryway. Al smiled at the decoration because he could imagine Veronica putting the ornamental piece together herself. She struck him as very creative and artistic. His presumptions had been confirmed when he saw her in action at work. She had a habit of picking out the most eye appealing items for the restaurant. Even the way she spoke sounded like poetry to him. She had a way of lacing her words together in such a manner that it sounded like verse of a love song.

Al expected the startled look in her eyes. She looked simply beautiful. Part of her braided hair was pinned into a loose bun while the remaining rested about her shoulders. She wore a pair of blue and white striped drawstring pants with white tank top and a blue cardigan. He could tell that she had just showered because he could smell the fresh scent of the soap and her skin held an after shower glow.

"Mr. Carter? What are you doing here?" She looked like a deer caught in the headlights.

"I had to see you Veronica." He stated as if his showing up at her door were a natural thing. "I told you before that my name to you is Al or Alejandro, either one I don't care. However Mr. Carter is not permitted." Veronica let out an exasperated breath and stepped aside to let Al enter her apartment. Before he tracked mud and dirt over her carpet Veronica instructed him to remove his boots. He did so silently while taking in the décor of her medium sized apartment.

Like many apartments in the area hers featured plain blank white walls, neutral toned carpeting, plenty of natural lighting from an abundance of windows, and old fashioned steam radiators. Veronica's personal style was reflected in every piece in her apartment. She had an overstuffed ivory colored sofa and love seat, a simple oak wood dinning set and shelves filled with CD jewel cases. There was a large antique Asian sewing table being used as a coffee table in the middle of the living room area and atop it was a lead crystal bowl filled with candy.

Veronica took his coat and walked to the hall closet to hang it. Her mind was going a thousand miles per minute. *What is he doing here? I can't believe he's here. I let him in for Christ's sake! Shit, shit, shit, shit, shit!* She decided that since he was there she could at least try to have a decent time with him.

"Would you like some hot chocolate? I was just about to make myself some." She found it amazing that she was able to not only sound, but also feel comfortable.

"Actually something a little stronger might be better."

"Check the fridge. I'm sure that you'll find something to your liking." Veronica took the opportunity to sneak away to her bedroom to assure that her laundry was put away. She had not been expecting any company so she utilized her time to catch up on some household chores. Because of that she had her under clothes lying on her bed.

"Is it alright if I open this bottle of wine?" Al asked standing in her bedroom doorway holding a bottle of wine that Veronica had purchased more than three months prior and never made attempt to consume. She stood transfixed by his stunning good looks. He had removed his sweatshirt and now stood in socks, sweatpants, and a white tee shirt. The undershirt fit to his well-maintained form and the pants hung leisurely from his slim hips. She had to catch her breath before she spoke. "Um yeah, yeah. That's fine. Just let me finish up in here and I'll join you in a minute." Al could see that the item she had in her hand was made of lace and knew that it was some of her personal items. He gave a sly smirk, nodded his head, and left Veronica to finish her duty at hand.

Veronica sat on her sofa while Al chose to partake in her carpeted floor. His own apartment had hard wood flooring so he thoroughly enjoyed that he could sit on hers.

"So what are you doing spending the holiday alone, Veronica?" Her named rolled off his tongue like honey. Her head was swirling with his presence but she was determined not to succumb to his seduction.

"I suppose I could ask you the same question. My mother is in Florida with our family and unlike her I couldn't take being around them for more than a few hours." She stated bitterly.

"Don't care for your family?" The animosity she let slip out piqued his interest.

"I can't say that I don't care for them it's just we still have a lot of unresolved issues in my view, and I'm unwilling to pretend that my family treated me and my mom with kindness and love." She drew her legs into her body and pulled the crochet throw that sat next to her over her lower body.

"Tell me about it." Al persuaded. He liked to hear her voice, but more than that he wanted to know as much about her as he could get her to disclose.

"My mother had me when she was sixteen. My grandparents were less than enthusiastic about it and they sent her away to a maternity home to have me." She stopped speaking and for a moment Al held his breath waiting for her to continue. When she didn't he let his breath out. He didn't want to push her so he changed the subject.

"Well you have the rest of the week off, what are your plans?"

"Nothing much really, the basketball game starts in a few minutes. I've been looking forward to it then I'm going to the Browns game on Sunday after church." Al was impressed. He hadn't picked Veronica to be a sports fan but apparently she was. Though his better judgment told him not to ask he had to know. "Who are you going to the game with?" He knew he didn't sound casual and he wasn't about to try.

"No one. A girl can like football can't she?"

"Of course, it's just that I kinda want to go with you." He confessed.

"I only have one ticket, and I spent a lot of time and money on a ticket broker to get it. I got club seating." Al hated to deflate her bubble and tell her that his family had season tickets in a private loge, but he wanted to spend as much time with her as possible.

"It doesn't matter. I have tickets." He got up off the floor and sat next to her on the sofa. "Will you allow me the honor and attend the game with me?" Veronica's conscience ate away at her and begged her to say no, but she conceded and nodded in agreement.

"You walked over here?" Veronica's curiosity was engaged. Until that moment she hadn't cared that Al obviously knew what building she lived in, that information was in her personal file at work and just about anyone could access that much but she hadn't listed an apartment number. "Yeah I walked. You don't live too far from me. I needed to get out of my place for a while and I wound up here." He told her.

"How did you know what apartment I lived in?"

"I asked one of your neighbors a few days ago."

"A few days ago?" Veronica pulled her body away from Al's that at that point was touching hers. With his revelation she became instantly uncomfortable. Al felt her retreat and refused to give into her apprehensions. The space that she'd created between them, Al quickly closed by moving closer to her.

"Are you stalking me or something? What the hell do you mean a few days ago?" Veronica was furious with him but even more with herself for actually being flattered by his behavior.

"No I'm not. I've known where you live for a while. I just hadn't come up with the courage to come in the building to see you until today. I sat in my apartment and thought that I was going crazy. I couldn't get you off my mind Veronica." The pleading of his voice broke down her defenses and she allowed him to wrap his arms around her.

"I don't appreciate you sneaking around trying to gather information on me. Next time you wanna know something about me just ask."

"I think I can do that." He wanted to ask her why she seemed so jumpy around men, but thought better of it. He was enjoying himself in her company and would just as soon drink poison than ruin the moment. They sat in silence for a few more minutes before Veronica spoke.

"The game comes on in a minute. Are you going to stay and watch it with me or do you have plans with your family?"

"No plans at all. They are all in Brazil until after the New Year."

"Why aren't you with them?"

"Because I wanted to be with you." For what seemed to be common action, Veronica's mind had become nothing more than mush. Sitting next to her, holding her body in his arms sat a man. A man who brought out the best and worst in her. A man who in a matter of hours uncovered what had taken her years to bury away. She knew that the more she resisted the more she was pulled to him, and that frightened her.

Al and Veronica watched the double header together and shared a dinner of traditional Greek fare prepared by Nick. He'd asked her to share Christmas dinner with him and his brother, but she felt that he and his family needed time together. It was no secret amongst them that Nick was in love with Veronica's mother. It was just unknown why

76

they were not together. Veronica speculated that there had been an affair involving her mother and Nick long before Tammy revealed the truth to her.

Veronica awoke to find herself curled into Al's embrace on her sofa. She glanced at the clock on the cable box and realized that it had become very late and while the neighborhood was relatively safe, she didn't want him walking home in the snow at that hour.

Veronica shook Al's arm to wake him but he barely stirred. Without knowing what came over her Veronica adjusted her position so that she was facing him and began to place soft kisses on his face. Moving around his face she made her way to his ears and neck, once she began to suckle on them she got a reaction from him. His eyes fluttered open and he took hold of her mouth with his own. For what felt like hours, they kissed and touched like teenagers in heat.

Al slid his hand into the waist band of Veronica's house pants only to find that she did not wear any panties and the discovery only intensified his yearning. Hating to have to break their bond Al rose off the sofa and lifted Veronica into his arms and carried her to her bedroom.

Al placed Veronica's body in the middle of her large bed and removed her cardigan placing gentle kisses along her bare shoulders. Veronica shivered from his touch and tried to place her mouth on his once more but he stopped her and continued his oral work on her body. She felt like screaming but when she opened her mouth nothing came out, not even her own breath escaped her lips. He found that her nipples had hardened when he searched under the cotton garment of her tank top with his powerful hands. Veronica finally let air into her lungs when he caught her peaked nipple between his fingers.

Al looked at Veronica's face and realized that she wasn't sure about them. Her eyes held conflicting emotions of lust and terror. At that moment he decided that he could not continue. He was a gentleman and although he had not done so in the past, he intended to carry himself as one then. More than anything he wanted to keep on his road of action but he would not compromise her reservations for his own selfish wants.

"Veronica I can't do this to you." He was honest with his statement. He cared for the doe eyed woman staring back at him and he was going to prove it to her.

"Do what to me?" She was indignant but couldn't falsify her satisfaction in his decision.

"First, I won't have sex with you again without protecting you, and two, I have feelings for you that I want to make sure that you are fully aware of before we do this again." Veronica simply nodded in agreement. Without another word from either of them Al drew Veronica into a spoon position and lay next to her for the duration of the night.

While sleep came peacefully for Al, Veronica had no such luck. She lay awake in his arms for most of the night. She kept replaying his statement in her mind. She hadn't realized until he said it. They had unprotected intercourse and if her calculations were correct she was close to two weeks late. Seeing how she could set a watch to her period she knew that it meant only one thing. She was carrying his child.

****

The next day Al returned to his apartment alone after much pleading with Veronica to come with him. She'd said that she already had plans to meet with her friend Renee and that she'd try to call him later that day. While the fact that she had plans with Renee was true she only told a half-truth. Her lunch date with Renee was to be an over night trip to Pennsylvania.

The day after Christmas always had good bargain shopping at the outlet stores in the neighboring state. Once Veronica and Renee had made their way to the outlet mall with just a few hundred dollars from Christmas gifts and purchased articles that would have easily exceeded their limits at regular retail price. What Renee and Al didn't know was that Veronica was going to use the trip as a means to purchase maternity clothing.

Almost ten years prior Veronica sat in a recovery room with a tear stained face and made two promises to her self. The first one she'd broken. She had once again gone and had premarital sex. The second was that she would never abort another child. While redemption from her self for herself seemed far, far away. She decided in the car on the way to Pennsylvania, that her unborn child would not pay for her sins.

Chapter Ten

It was less than a week from the restaurant's grand opening on Valentines Day and everyone involved was antsy. Chef Brasilio was waiting on confirmation for the shipment of Chilean Sea Bass and seemed as if he would explode if any one spoke to him.

Veronica was more than unsuccessful at trying to hide her nervousness. She wasn't sure if she could blame her queasiness on her work or the child growing within her belly. She knew that she looked out of sorts when she came to work two days prior with her hair undone and wearing casual clothing like the rest of her co-workers. If there was one thing Veronica would not be accused of it was coming to work looking amuck.

George had approached her and inquired if she was all right. "I'm fine. I know that we have a lot of work to do and some of it won't be pretty so I decided to put on clothes that were more fitting to manual labor. That's all, don't worry."

"All right Veronica. I'd hate to see you ill at our expense. Everyone has really put forth one hundred percent and I don't want to see all of you guys efforts go to waste."

"Waste?" She questioned "This is going to be the grandest opening the city has seen and more importantly this will put CaSa at the top of the list for entertainment development. I can't wait until things really take off." The joy gleaming in her eyes melted George's heart. She was everything his cousin Nick said that she was. Veronica discovered George and Nick grew up together and were distant cousins the day she revealed to Nick that she was with child. Renee was the only other person that she'd told.

Nick had told George to keep an eye on his girl for him. Nick had no intentions on spilling Veronica's secret to his family member but George proved to be a formidable opponent and got Nick to admit that he had vested feelings for the young woman. Nick told George how he was still in love with Veronica's mother and how he has watched Veronica grow into an exceptional woman. He just couldn't stand seeing her getting harmed because she refused to give into her condition.

Nick made George promise not to mention his knowledge of her situation to her for he knew that she would never trust him with such information again. George broke his promise to Nick when Veronica's feeble attempts at concealing her vulnerability brought her to tears.

When Veronica walked into the restaurant that day she hadn't expected to see Al waiting for her in her office. They hadn't spoken since they argued upon her return from Pennsylvania. Veronica had not called Al the day after Christmas as she lead him to believe that she would and Al was furious with her for having him so worried. Al was waiting for her at her apartment building entrance and exploded with anger at seeing her walk up with her friend and plenty of shopping bags in tow.

Veronica felt that he overreacted and told him so. From that point the argument got even more heated until Renee stepped in and refereed. All of Veronica's anger returned at seeing Al's leisurely appraisal of her. He had a way of making her feel naked although she was fully clothed.

"Is there some thing I can help you with Mr. Carter?" She raised her eyebrow in a questioning manner.

"You can start by calling me Al, Veronica." He deliberately crossed his arms and sunk further into his chair to show that he had no notions of leaving. Veronica had been avoiding him at all cost and he was not going to stand for it any longer. He'd reacted harshly towards her for not calling him when she'd only promised to try to call and he was sorry for that. However on more than one occasion he'd tried to extend his apologies to the stubborn woman but she'd constantly denied him a moment alone.

"Mr. Carter, I have no misgivings about the formality of our relationship and I hope that you don't either." Veronica was feeling physically weak she had been unable to keep anything solid down for weeks and her sleepless nights only escalated her poor condition. Al noted that she lost weight and her skin hadn't the luster he'd grown to adore. He knew that Veronica could keep her feelings bottled up in a very public manner but he wasn't so sure that her appearance was caused totally by his rude behavior.

"What's going on Veronica? You seem a little out of it."

"I'm not out of anything except patience for you and your way too unpredictable attitude."

"Unpredictable?" If anyone was unpredictable it was she. She was the one who let him take her virginity, in his office no less. She was the one who let him in a little one moment only to shut him out the next. He was fed up with Veronica Parker and he told her so.

"I am so sick of you Veronica. You need to grow up a little! You act as if you're so goddamned mature but you are nothing but a scared little girl afraid of everything! Why? Why Veronica?" He was standing and at that moment Veronica became fully aware of his intimidating height.

"I'm not afraid of any goddamn thing and least of all I'm not afraid of you!" Because she was so enraged she didn't pay attention to her lunch churning in her stomach until it was too late and she was vomiting in her wastebasket by her desk. Not sure what to do Al just stood by wide- eyed and watched as Veronica wretched and gagged her way through an uncomfortable situation.

Al moved to help Veronica into her seat. Even though her head was spinning and she felt as if she was about to faint, Veronica mustered enough strength to push Al away. "Get the hell off me you asshole!" He felt as if he had that coming but was still hurt by the vile words she flung at him.

"Veronica let me help you, please."

"I don't want your blasted help!" Her stomach felt as if someone had taken a vacuum tube, shoved it down her throat, and flicked the on switch to super suction. She desperately needed to leave but would not give Al the satisfaction of seeing her retreat.

"Leave Alejandro!" She ordered.

"I will not, my love." He replied.

"What do you want from me, Alejandro? Because whatever it is I can not supply you." Her pleading eyes were granted their reprieve when he moved away from her and allowed her to move unassisted.

"I want you Veronica Parker."

"Well you can't have me Alejandro Carter." She let out breathlessly as she took her seat.

"I can and I will, that you can count on Veronica." Al stood, turned on his heels and headed towards the office entrance. With his hand on the door handle Al turned in Veronica's direction and spoke. "Veronica as your friend I am advising you to go home and get some rest as your boss I am hoping that you'll take the advice of your friend and leave because it seems that you've come down with something and I'd hate to see the rest of my staff catch it." With that he opened the door and stormed out, leaving Veronica to stare at his retreating back.

A few minutes later George walked into her office to find Veronica crying. His heart went out to her but he knew that her problem was one that she would have to face and work out on her own.

"Go home Ronnie. We'll manage for a few days without you."

"George I'm not sick. I don't need to go home, I'm just a little nervous and tired from all the hours I'm putting in, I'll be fine." George's patience had run out and he was not about to let Veronica work herself into a miscarriage.

"Ronnie!" He boomed startling Veronica enough to make her give him full attention. "You will not carry a child and continue to behave the way you are. Go home!" He had no concern for her shocked reaction to his admission.

"Nick told you?" She had suspected that Nick revealed the tender information to George so that he could keep an eye on her. However she didn't think that George would compromise Nick's confidence.

"Yes he told me. He also told me that you would not reveal the identity of the father, but listening to you and Al's conversation I could just about guess who it is."

"You heard us?" Things were going to fast for Veronica to latch on to one solid piece of information.

"I couldn't help it. I was coming to tell you to leave but I stopped outside your door when I heard you and him yelling at one another. I walked away before he came out. It didn't matter, he came and found me and said that you were to leave and not return until you were feeling better." Veronica's face had taken on a crimson shade. George was worried that she might send her blood pressure to unseen heights.

"That son of a bitch. How dare he..."

"No Veronica. How dare you. Have you even told him? Let me answer that, No you haven't. And no matter your personal differences he deserves to know."

"He doesn't deserve a damned thing from me. He'll have to know eventually when I start to show." She said defiantly crossing her arms.

"Al is a good man and he should know. That's all I'm discussing with you about this matter. As far as I'm concerned it is none of my concern, however your health and well-being are. Go home." The finality in his voice warned her not to argue.

Veronica left for the rest of the day and decided to visit her mother at work. She'd yet to tell Tammy Parker that she was to become a grandmother and she was sure that the news was going to be received with a joyous response. The other thing that she was sure of was that her mother was going to agree with Nick, Renee, and George and say that she had an obligation to tell Al of his impeding fatherhood.

****

Opening day had arrived and the CaSa offices were busy with last minute paperwork, phone calls, and preparations. Veronica had returned to work the day after she was sent home much to the chagrin of Al and George. Al tried to stop her from entering her office but she politely warned him of treading the line of misconduct and causing a scene.

Everything seemed to be in place for the opening. Many Cleveland and Ohio politicians had confirmed their reservations, a few of the large business owners were bringing their wives in for the special banquet being held in the larger half of the restaurant, and the press was setting up to conduct interviews for their respective pieces for the evening news.

There had never been such an event for the city and everyone was giddy with excitement. Veronica and the rest of the staff had coordinated their attire to fit the color scheme of the serving and kitchen staff. Veronica was the only woman who opted to ware a deep red; the rest chose the option of standard black. Although she had lost some weight, the gown she chose accented Veronica's voluptuous contours. She knew that her time was running out and she wasn't going to be able to conceal her pregnancy from Al much longer, but figured that it would have to wait until after they both weren't so preoccupied.

Veronica arrived at Four Corner's just after four in the afternoon. The only other people who were there was Chef Brasilio and the kitchen staff. The opening was scheduled for six and the serving staff was due to come in at four thirty, so Veronica had some time to review her schedule of events. She didn't notice Al sitting at a table in the far corner of the restaurant watching her. The lighting was fairly dim in the main eating area to set a specific mood.

Unless one was very close to a table it was hard to tell whom if anyone was sitting there.

Al closely followed Veronica with his eyes until she was no longer in sight and then he just stared at the last spot she stood. He was so sorry for the way he berated her but she was so stubborn and so was he. He had to admit to himself that he liked her spunk and attitude; they were some of her best traits. He also had to admit that they were also some of her most annoying qualities.

Once the restaurant was up and running, CaSa's involvement would become less significant and Al would only see Veronica on a limited basis. The company's next big project would be a Downtown restaurant/Jazz club in Cincinnati. Al's older brother Simon would be heading that project. Al had elected to stay in Cleveland to see Four Corners through its first year while working on a few other small-scale projects around town.

CaSa had won the development accounts for the new steak house restaurant at the zoo, the new disco near a Hospital, and the renovation and new management of an exclusive country club in an upscale lakeshore sub-division. Four Corners was Al's baby. He had worked the East Coast for two years and actually looked forward to his opportunity to get out of New York.

At twenty-eight, Al had worked for his family business for nearly five years. Until the recent past that work had been done at a distance from his parent's and brothers watchful eye. Since deciding to move back to his father's hometown Al had begun to feel the tension of being around his parents creep back into his body.

Because of his intelligence and sensitivity, Al believed that his parents, more specifically his father, thought it their duty to make his life a living hell. He felt they had a habit of making him feel inferior. He sat in the comfortable muted lights of the restaurant and recalled the day he entered high school.

"Alejandro, I want you to be careful at school. Those children will be much older than you." His mother warned in rapid Portuguese. Mariana Sa-Carter made it a point for her children to be fluent in both Spanish and Portuguese.

"Mama do not worry, I will not get hurt." The young Al replied. He was thirteen and up until that point was not allowed to skip any levels in school, much to his protest. Elementary and middle school bored him to the point of torture, but his parents felt that he needed to socialize amongst children his own age.

"You are right my little man. You will be fine." She agreed in English. Al left his mother's company and joined his father in his study to tell him good-by before he left for school. Al knocked softly on the solid oak door before entering.

"Dad, I'll be leaving soon. I just wanted to say bye."

"Come in son. I want to talk to you before you leave." Simon Sr. sat at his desk in casual clothing. His hair had begun to gray around the temples but other than that he still maintained a youthful appearance.

"Son I want you to know that I don't agree with you going in to the tenth grade. I only conceded because your mother would have it no other way." Simon paused and gave his son a once over. At the time Al had a very slender and rangy build, since then he firmly filled out. Simon Sr. continued, "I have my reservations about all of this because you are still so, so...I don't know, but I do know that you are not ready for such a step, at least not emotionally."

"Dad I understand how you feel, but I don't think that it's possible for me to stay at this pace. It's too slow for me."

"Books can not be your only solace in life son. And I am afraid that you will not be able to make the right decisions in life when the time comes." Will you ever? Al asked to him self. "Son I just wish you would reconsider?" Al's father had hoped that his last statement sounded the way he wanted it to but it still came out as a question. Al feeling on the spot replied, "Dad I just want to be able to go and do what I like and that happens to be going to school."

"Okay Son, go on and have a good day." After that conversation Al chose to spend half a school year as a junior before he couldn't take it anymore and moved on to be a senior. Al never felt as if his father saw him competent enough to make his own decisions. Even as an adult Simon Carter Sr. second guessed Al's choices or tried to make them for him.

Landis, the charismatic host shook Al by the shoulder and brought him out of his trance.

"Hey man, wake up. You've got a place to run cause I ain't doin' it for you"

Al smiled at the attractive young man. Landis was a very witty and understanding twenty-seven year old. Landis sported tiny cornrows, a trim goatee, and a small diamond in his right ear. The young man had a killer smile and was very well built. It was obvious that he frequented time at the gym and his diligence was rewarded in the form of a muscular five foot eleven frame.

"I'm sure that you could handle it Landis. You're the pro, I'm just along for the ride." Al enjoyed talking to Landis, he was able to relax around him and be him self.

"Ha! Boss man, you know this is your show. Just make it a good one."

"Hey don't I always." Al flashed his subordinate a grateful smile, stood, and buttoned his tuxedo jacket. "Landis, thanks man. I needed a smile."

"Anytime Boss Man, anytime." Landis made his way back across the dinning room floor to his post by the elevator bank. Al said a silent prayer for the successful opening of his first solo project. With it he could finally prove his competency to his father.

Chapter Eleven

Veronica ignored the rumbling in her belly from her obvious hunger. She realized she had not eaten since early in the day and it was well past eight in the evening. She figured that she'd just continue on as she normally would however, she was not in a normal situation. She was pregnant and her actions could not only harm her but the child she was carrying as well.

There were still many reservations left to come in and most of the administrative staff had left for the evening. Only Veronica, George, the Bar manger Marge, and Al remained. The restaurant activity had yet to die down and no one expected it to do so before midnight. Just after nine o'clock while Veronica was giving Landis a much-needed break, in walked a beautiful red head escorted by an equally alluring blond man.

Veronica greeted the woman with a warm smile and took note of her protruding stomach. Veronica had to look up to the statuesque woman to address her because her six-foot height required it.

"Welcome to Four Corners, How may I help you?"

"By showing us our table, two for Riley." The posh inflection in her voice made Veronica internally cringe. Almost instantly she detested the woman standing before her and so did the child she was carrying. Veronica's stomach knotted as she formed all of her strength to keep her face neutral. "Right this way please." Veronica turned right into Al's chest and he had to grab her by the arms to keep her from loosing her balance. "Please excuse me, Mr. Carter."

The fact that Al's gaze never left Samantha's smug expression was completely lost on Veronica.

"No apology necessary, Veronica. Sam, how are you?" This time Veronica did notice the silent exchange between the two and was chilled to her core by the look on Al's face.

"Al, I'm as well as can be expected for a woman five months pregnant." For the first time Al noticed her condition. He was flabbergasted by the news; five months would mean there was a possibility that he was the father. Samantha must have read his thought process because before he had a chance to speak in rebuttal she added, "I know that this is a shock to you hon, but look at it this way, now you'll have that child you said that you wanted."

Al's mouth dropped open. Disbelief could not describe what he was feeling at that moment. Samantha had walked into his place of business and deliberately dropped a bomb on him, she was pregnant and she said that the child was his. Although it was a tense situation Al kept his composure and said to Veronica "Please show Miss Riley and her date to their table Veronica and please see that they receive complimentary dessert, it's obvious that she has reason to celebrate." He turned and walked away without another word.

Veronica was in a state of mind that words could only skim and not fully describe. Her mind went numb and her legs felt like she had just ran a marathon. Until Miss Riley delivered her earth shattering news Veronica had told herself that she was going to tell Al of her pregnancy the next day, however with the tall red head's news she wasn't so sure that was her best option.

After seating Samantha and her extraordinarily good looking date Veronica wished them a pleasant evening and turned to leave but Samantha grabbed her by the wrist.

"Listen; don't get your hopes up about your boss."

"Excuse me?" Veronica had no clue what Samantha was referring to. Samantha excused herself to her date and asked Veronica to show her to the ladies room. Veronica knew instinctively that it was all a very bad idea but she felt the need to humor the gorgeous woman. Once in the rest room, Samantha took her time primping in the mirror before she spoke.

"So, you have a thing for Al do you?" Her words were spiked with knowing and malice.

"I really don't have the slightest idea as to what you are talking about, Miss Riley."

"I saw the way that you looked at him and the way your faced dropped when I told him about his child." Veronica had to confess to her self that she was crushed upon hearing the news. Samantha continued, "as I said before, don't get your hopes up, he's mine and so is this." She rubbed her rounded belly in a circular motion.

"If that child is his why'd you wait so long to tell him?" This was the same question she was sure any person who knew about her child could ask.

"Not that this is any of your concern, but I've miscarried before and I wanted to make sure that this child would get past the risk period." Samantha sat on a cushioned bench across from Veronica who'd sat down due to weariness.

"I told you out there, don't get your hopes up, he's mine." Veronica could tell her adversary was accustomed to having her way and getting what she wanted and Veronica wasn't sure she could compete with a woman such as her.

"My hopes are of no consequence to you. If he is yours then by all means please claim what rightfully belongs to you. But leave me out of it, I have no beef with you, so don't create any." Determined not to let Samantha get in another word, Veronica moved quickly and left Samantha alone in the bathroom.

Veronica had already determined that after Landis returned from his break, she was going to head home well before Samantha walked into the restaurant. Because of the escalated situation Veronica found herself immersed in, she opted to leave before Landis returned. She found a server and instructed them to cover the post for the remaining five minutes of Landis's break.

Moving quickly Veronica changed shoes and made a quiet exit via the staircase. Before she knew it she had went down twenty flights and was now exhausted. She left the staircase and walked into the receptionist area of a law firm that rented that floor.

Veronica found a chair by the windows facing the lake and sat down. She sat there for about a half-hour not really thinking but drifting off into a space where thought didn't exist. When she finally came back to reality and focused on why she was sitting there in the dark, she began to cry. Until that moment she hadn't realized that she cared so much for Al. For the life of her she couldn't figure out what made her hurt so bad when it came to him. Maybe it was the way he tapped into her feelings, her fears, and her joys. Maybe it was the fact that she was carrying his child. Maybe it was because she'd allowed him to get closer to her than any other man. Whatever the reason, however it happened, she was in love with Al, and there was nothing she could do about it.

****

The banging on her door jolted Veronica out of her sleep. She'd fallen asleep on her sofa while still in her two-piece gown. She looked at her watch and saw that it was a completely improper time for an unannounced visitor, which meant that Al was the only person who could be on the other side of the door.

"Go away!" She yelled from the sofa. Veronica was in no mood to fight with Al. The insistent pounding continued. "Let me in Veronica." He ordered from the other side of the barrier.

"No! Now go away and stop banging on the goddamn door!"

"I'll kick it in if I have to, so you better open up!"

"Don't te..." her words were cut off by the loud sound of Al ramming his shoulder into the door. *The crazy bastard is really trying to break my door down! I do not believe him!*

Frustrated and scared that one of her neighbors might call the authorities Veronica opened her door just as Al was about to put all of his weight into one last shove that was sure to bring her door down. She tried to move out his way to no avail and he shoved her into the hallway wall and they both toppled over with him landing atop her.

Luckily neither were harmed but Al had Veronica trapped on her hall floor.

"Let me up you jackass." She hissed while trying to squirm from beneath him. Al pushed the entry door closed with his foot as he adjusted his positioning to secure her even more under his mass.

"No." He stated just before he covered her mouth with his own. Veronica screamed only to have it die between their tongues. He grabbed her fisted hands and held them above her head so she couldn't pound on him any longer. Veronica hated that her body was reacting to his advances.

Al broke his probing kiss and traced his tongue along her bare collarbone down to the succulent well between her luscious breasts. Veronica moaned and Al continued to please her body as only he seemed to know how. He loosened the grip he had on her wrist and brought her arms around his neck. He rolled to his side and in a split second was standing and carrying Veronica to her bedroom. He turned on one of the bedside lamps once he placed her in the middle of the bed and asked her in Spanish to open her closed eyes.

"I want you to see me." He continued in the roman-tic language. Veronica tentatively opened her eyes and looked at the man who fathered her unborn child. He was wearing an impeccable Armani tuxedo that fit his form like it was made just for him, and knowing Al that was not impossible. His eyes had paled and now looked menacing. The set of his jaw had hardened and caused the vein on the side of his neck to pop out some. At that instant all Veronica wanted to do was wash away his pain. She wanted to turn herself into an emotional sponge and soak up all of his confusion and hurt.

She extended her hand to him and he happily accepted it. She brought him to her mouth and began a slow yet forcible kiss. Al placed his hand on her stomach and Veronica flinched and stiffened. Hoping he didn't notice her reaction she grabbed his hand and guided it to her breast. Al began undoing the gold buttons lining the front of the satin garment.

"Turn the light off please." Veronica was sure that if the light was on and she could see his face that she would stop her self from continuing. She didn't want to stop. Al turned off the light by the bed and straddled her body in the process.

Al began placing fluttering kisses down the middle of her torso as he undid each button. Once the last button was undone he returned to her quivering lips and traced a path over them with his tongue. Unlike their first encounter, Veronica was fully aware of Al's desire to have her open her mouth and she obliged. Al partook in her sweetness and could have sworn that he was going to explode from the exhilaration.

Veronica broke their passionate kiss so she could catch her breath and help him out of his clothing. The pants of the suit fit his slim waist perfectly and the cut of the shirt left only preliminaries to the imagination. Al was built beautifully. He possessed very powerful arms and legs that only someone who ran frequently could claim. His citrus scented cologne made Veronica's mind whirl in its spell.

Before Veronica could react, she felt her skirt being removed. Al's hands roved over her lower body like she was a rare sculpture. She was so overwhelmed by his touch that she tried to push his hands away, only to have her own hands pinned to her sides by him.

Al wasted little time in searching for and finding her love cavern, once there he started a slow love making with his tongue and sent uncontrollable shivers through his ladylove's body. Veronica called Al's name numerous times before she went sailing in to an ocean of pleasure, the sea of climatic turbulence.

Once his thirst was quenched Al made about shedding the remainder of his clothing. He grabbed Veronica's knees and gently separated them. Supporting himself on his arms Al entered Veronica's body with one staggering thrust. Veronica cried out to God and dug her nails into his back. Al's passion was sent into overdrive from the divine pain she caused his skin.

Al thrust in and out of the tight tunnel that was Veronica for what seemed like an eternity. Veronica crashed and was brought out of pleasant darkness more times than she could count. Light from the street lamp illuminated Al's face and the intensity consuming his eyes. His forehead and face were covered with a shimmering sheen of perspiration. Veronica could feel his member grow even more swollen and knew that his climax was near. She reached up and ran her fingers through his dark hair and pressed her mouth to his. It was his undoing; Al could hold on no longer and let his reservations, his pleasure, and his pain flow into the woman beneath him.

Veronica left their embrace after a few minutes and went to run her self a bath. She thought that Al was fast asleep when she entered the hot water but found she was mistaken when she opened her eyes to find him standing over her naked as the day he was born.

"I thought you were sleeping." She said and re-closed her eyes and leaned back onto the bath pillow.

"I was but when you got out of bed I woke up." He was mesmerized by her pure beauty. Her skin glowed from the mixture of oil and bubble bath she'd placed in the water. "Where's your sponge?" He asked while he sat on the edge of the tub. She searched around in the water, found the sponge, and silently offered the requested item to him. They sat silently as Al washed her back. He dipped the sponge into the aromatic water and let it trickle down her back several times before he'd completely satisfied his eyes with the show.

"Take down your braids, I like to see them down." He'd had many sleepless nights due to his thinking about her head full of braids blowing around wildly in the wind, utterly unobstructed and free.

"I will when I get out of the tub, I don't want them to get wet."

"Why?" He was confused and it showed in his response.

"Because they are a hassle to dry and I'm too tired to go through that."

"Okay, no need to get your back up. It was just an honest question." He was right it was a simple question and she'd snapped at him, but contrary to what he thought she felt she had more than cause to be upset with him and his simple question had retargeted her anger.

"It's not just a simple question. It's validation that this, you and me, is not going to work. We are two different people, with different problems, different backgrounds, different races." She let the last word trail off into the air.

"Don't go there Veronica, because you and I both know that race has nothing to do with our being together, at least it has no bearing on what I feel. Sure I've noticed that you and I are not of the same pigmentation, but..."

"You've noticed!" She interrupted, "there is nothing to just casually notice. I'm black and you are white, plain and simple. Moreover you come from a lot of money and I do not, but what's even more relevant, you are about to have a child and I refuse to be a part of anyone's 'Baby Mama Drama'."

"Baby Mama Drama?" He asked.

"Yes. See, that's exactly what I'm talking about. I don't want to have to explain everything to you..." she stopped when he placed his finger to her mouth in an attempt to silence her.

"I know what the term means, and there will be none of that."

"You obviously don't take time to get to know the women you sleep with, because Miss Riley has already staked her claim." Veronica leaned back into the tub. The water had begun to cool and she wanted to savor what little warmth was left. Al had sat on the floor by then because the edge of the claw foot tub had grown uncomfortable.

"Did she say something to you?"

"Of course she did, but that's neither here nor there. The fact of the matter is you and she have unresolved issues and now another issue grows inside her. I can't and won't compete with her or your child." Al clenched his jaw to keep from letting his resentment for Samantha spew from his mouth. His dispute with her had nothing to do with Veronica and he was determined to keep it that way. He'd made a promise to behave as the gentleman that he was raised to be and he would not let Samantha Riley get him to break it.

"You will not compete for anything that you already have." Veronica could tell that Al was more than angry because his eyes had become so dark that they almost looked black. Not willing to anger him any more with talk of events that he hadn't the chance to diffuse, she closed the subject and all other means of discussion.

"Let's go to bed, we can talk about this in the morning. I'm not due in until noon tomorrow so I'll have time."

"Fine, I'll join you in a moment after I shower."

Veronica left the tub and toweled off. She had a feeling that things between her an Al were far from the point of resolution and that scared her.

Chapter Twelve

Tammy eyed her daughter suspiciously over the rim of her coffee mug. She knew that Al had made an unannounced visit to her offspring the evening before and she also knew that Veronica was not giving her all the details of what transpired between the two of them. Be that as it may, she was not entirely comfortable with the way things were going for her child.

"So I trust that everything went well at the opening last night?" Tammy wanted to ask her more than that but figured she stood better chances of getting a snowball not to melt in hell than to get her to reveal any dealings between her daughter and Al.

"Fine", was Veronica's monosyllabic answer. Tammy was just about to attempt a deeper prodding into the source of Veronica's melancholy mood when Renee burst through the diner entrance and made her way back to their table. The diner was a lot bigger that it's competition across the tracks. Nick's Place had about 3,000 square feet of total space including the storage, restrooms, and small banquet facility occupying the basement. The diner had once been an urban clothing store, a teashop, and an Arabic-dining club. However none of the previous renters enjoyed the monetary success that Nick's had. He had relocated his diner from the lobby of a nearby hospital when the county had shut down its emergency and ICU services. Nick saw the shut down as divine intervention and quickly took hold of an opportunity to expand his operations.

Even though the space was quite large no one could deny Renee an opportunity to make an entrance. Renee dwarfed her best friend with her lean five foot eight height. She had long wavy reddish brown hair that flaunted natural golden blonde streaks. Her French vanilla colored skin left no room to mistake her Creole ancestry. Renee, like Veronica, was fluent in Spanish but also claimed knowledge of the French and Portuguese dialects.

"Hola, Chicas!" Renee greeted as she sat in the empty seat awaiting her arrival. Veronica and Tammy returned their responses in similar tongue. The conversation continued in the native language of Tammy's Puerto Rican raised father. Julius Parker was raised in Puerto Rico by his Uncle and Aunt after his parent's tragic murder when he was just a few months old in the racially divided south.

Julius was found screaming and crying from hunger and neglect while his mother and father's bodies sat in the front seat with bullets in each of their heads. He never had the opportunity to avenge their deaths. The criminals were never brought to trial and Julius was taken to Puerto Rico where he lived until he moved to Florida to attend college.

"Well, tell me how did the opening go?" Renee asked, turning her attention to her friend. Veronica gave Renee the same answer that she gave her mother, "fine."

Renee and Tammy exchanged knowing looks then Renee proceeded to pick up where Tammy had left off. "What do you mean fine, this opening had been all you could talk about the past few weeks, so I know it had to be more than fine?" Veronica knew that she would not be able to get out the diner alive if she tried to make a quick escape for the door.

"It was alright I suppose. We had a small fire in the kitchen, one woman came in with her sister to find her husband sitting at a nearby table with his mistress, and Al's ex-girlfriend came in and told him that she's pregnant with his baby." Without looking up from her steak and mashed potatoes Veronica could sense that her mother and Renee's mouths were wide open and their jaws in their laps. A few silent moments passed before anyone spoke. Renee elected to be the first to speak.

"What?" it was the only thing that her mind could form to speak.

"I said that there was a small fire in the kitch..." Tammy grabbed her daughter's hand in effort to silence her. Tammy spoke next, "What ex-girlfriend? And what do you mean she's pregnant with his child?"

"Like I said she came to dinner last night big ass stomach and all, looking like miss lifestyles of the rich and privileged and announced in front of anyone who was listening that she was carrying his baby." She sat staring out the window for a few moments before she returned her thoughts to the present and the conversation she was having with her mother and Renee.

Tammy was at a lost for something appropriate to say and decided frankness was her best option. She knew that Veronica was holding something back and she wanted to know what it was and decided to find out what it was.

"What else, Veronica?"

"Nothing else, Mom." Veronica went back to picking at her mashed potatoes.

"You dare lie to me? Girl if you don't open your mouth and tell me what else is going on I swear I'll jump across this table and beat the living day lights out of you!" Renee had only seen Veronica's mother get so upset once before and that was when Veronica and she had thought it would be fun to cut school. They quickly learned that there was no fun in being caught hiding in the hall closet by Tammy Parker on her lunch break.

"Ma, listen if there were more I would tell you more, but since there isn't I have nothing to tell." Veronica's eyes began to water and she wanted nothing more at the moment than to get up and get away before the tears fell. Handing her a napkin Renee said, "If there's nothing else, why are you crying Ronnie?"

Veronica couldn't hold the tears any longer. She wailed for close to five minutes before she gained her composure. By that time Nick had come over to their table and sat down ready to listen to Veronica reveal her heart to them.

"Ronnie? It is okay, you know, all does not come easy in the heart. You tell us we are your family. You trust us, no?" Veronica shook her head in response. "Then you talk, we listen." Nick always had a way of getting Veronica to open up and talk out her feelings; this time was no exception.

"Well, I really don't know where to begin. I guess from the start is the best place. Each of you knows a portion of what's going on so I guess I'll have to tell you all from the beginning." Veronica recapped everything from how she and Al had met to her confrontation in the bathroom with Samantha Riley. "You mean the Life and Style columnist for the news paper, Samantha Riley?" Renee asked.

"The one and the same." Veronica confirmed.

Veronica had recognized Samantha the instant she entered Four Corners. Samantha's feline eyes had Veronica transfixed when she walked into the restaurant the day before. Samantha didn't fit the bill for a typical newspaper journalist. She was an attractive woman, a very attractive woman. She could have easily been a runway model but decided that she would pursue a career that required a lot more fortitude and guts than most accredited her to have.

"How far along is she?" Renee asked. Tammy and Nick exchanged glances that mirrored each other's concern for the young woman sitting across from them.

"It doesn't matter how far along she is, what's important is that he find out if it's his, I'm sure he didn't question you about the paternity of your child did he?" Tammy directed her inquiry at her Daughter.

"He still doesn't know." Veronica reluctantly confessed.

"What you mean he not know?" Nick was astonished to hear the news. Tammy had called him to ask if he knew about Veronica's pregnancy and about the identity of the father. At the time Nick was not aware of whom it was, only that Veronica was with child and that she had told the father of her condition.

"I mean what I said, he still doesn't know and to be perfectly honest I'm not sure I'm going to tell him."

"What?" Renee asked.

"He doesn't need to know, I'm not even sure I'm going to keep it."

"What?" Renee, Nick, and Tammy exclaimed in unison.

"Is that all you know how to say?" Veronica asked in frustration. Veronica had yet to disclose her thought pattern to the other table occupants until that moment.

"Not keep it, but Ronnie I thought that you said you'd never do that again?" Renee said as she grabbed her friend's hand and enveloped it in to her slender pale fingers. Renee's eyes welled with tears; she could not believe that Veronica was actually contemplating aborting another child. As if reading the horrid thoughts going through her dinner companion's minds, Veronica clarified her statement. "I mean after I have it, I might give it up for adoption."

"Oh no the hell you're not. Not my only Grandbaby. If that's the case give him or her to me." Tammy was less than pleased with Veronica even entertaining the thought of giving up her child. She'd raised her daughter to make strong and smart decisions and when she didn't do so she made sure that Veronica did not run away from the consequences.

"Ma, I just thought about it, not seriously, just as a maybe."

"Maybe what, Ronnie?" Nick asked. The knowing look on his face scared Veronica. He knew that she was afraid that Al would not want them, her and her child. She was afraid that things were moving to quickly and it seemed that they weren't slowing down. She was afraid of raising a child on her own; she was just plain scared. Al's words from weeks before rang in her head. All she could hear was him calling her a scared little girl.

"Maybe I can't do this, Maybe he'll say that my baby isn't his maybe, maybe...may..." Veronica let her jumbled thoughts take over and did what seem to come so easily for her since getting pregnant; cry.

****

"So you knocked her up?" Simon Jr. was accused of many things in his life, but being tactful was not one of them.

"Must you be so crass big brother?" Al asked.

"Must you be an idiot? You know dad is going to have a heart attack when he finds out. Why couldn't you have just married her and get it out the way?" Al had to restrain him self from leaping across his seat and slapping his brother.

"Is that what you did with Janet?" Al asked trying to get a grip on the surreal conversation between his brother and he.

"Absolutely, positively not! I fell in love with her the moment I laid eyes on her. She didn't feel the same way but you know how persuasive I am with the ladies." He arrogantly leaned back into his chair and made a production of lacing his hands behind his head.

"Well I'm so happy for you and your ego, but if I could be serious with you, I have a real problem." Al leaned forward and placed his right forearm on his khaki clad knee. "Samantha waited months, five goddamn months to be exact, to tell me that she's pregnant, what am I supposed to do?" He was grasping for a glimmer of hope and wisdom from his elder brother.

"I really can't offer to much little brother, I mean you are the one whose always saying that we should trust you to make you own decisions. Aren't you the one who said that we see you as emotionally incompetent and immature? So the question is not what I think you should do, it's what you think you should do? Now's not the time to retract your statement or where you stand." Al could see that his brother was finding humor in his pain but he could not deny his wisdom on the subject.

Simon Jr., like their father, felt that his brother was a little careless when it came to the matters of the heart but learned through experience that it was best to force Al to acknowledge and face his own demons, because holding his hand through tough situations always produced adverse results.

"I'm in love with Veronica Parker." Al said as if that were the solution to his problems. Simon was taken aback by Al's revelation, he had no clue the two were seeing each other let alone seriously enough for there to be talk of love.

"What do you mean? When did you two start seeing each other?"

"We're not, I mean not officially, I guess what you could call it is a serious friendship."

"Hold up, are you or are you not dating her?"

"If you mean do we go out to the movies and dinner, or if we have gone to events together as a couple, no I can't say that we have, but that doesn't mean that my feelings for her are less valid because we haven't" Simon had to grant his brother that much. He and Janet dated only a few months before he proposed and they wed less than a year after meeting, time vested was not a policy Carter men practiced. However, Al was not cut of the same cloth as Simon Jr. and his father. No matter how much Al argued the contrary, he was more sensitive and fragile than his father and brother, and that always seemed to be an area of concern for the family.

"So if you don't mind me asking, how do you know you love her if you haven't spent any real time with her?" Simon reached for the beer sitting on the bar behind them. The two decided to attend a basketball game together. The private loge was designed to fit twelve people but the visiting team wasn't very popular and thus the game attendance was a very low number by standards. The only reason Al had accepted his brother's offer to accompany him was because he needed something to occupy his mind.

"I can't think without her popping up into my head. She makes me crazy most times but I look forward to our confrontations, and I have this uncontrollable urge to protect her. She came to work sick a few days before Four Corners opened and all I wanted to do was nurse her but I felt like choking her out of her stubborn set of mind. Do you know I had to pull rank on her to get her to go home?" Simon had heard that the two had a heated argument a few days before the opening; he had gained access as to why with Al's explanation. Al continued, "I know you and Mom and Dad think that I'm a little foolish and unstable but I know what I feel, I love her. I love her to the point that it hurts. I lay awake at night thinking about her, wishing she were with me. I want to get to know her better but she wont let me. I think that we've crossed a threshold and she pulls back. I don't know what to do and now with Samantha's news."

The desperation in Al's voice caused Simon to take his eyes away from the game and pay full attention to his brother. His heart went out to him, he knew that Al hadn't intended on getting Samantha pregnant, but because he had, Al had to face the drummer and step up to his responsibility.

"Al listen, this is all a shock but you had better do something and do it soon. You have a lot to do and you have to do it soon, her due date is quickly approaching."

"I know and Veronica is aware of the situation so I'd better figure something out. There's something else that I haven't told you yet." Al said tentatively.

"What?" Simon asked.

"I slept with Veronica."

"I figured as much, but what's the problem?" Simon detected that the situation was far more complicated than he'd first perceived from the sound of his brother's voice.

"I slept with her the day she came in for her interview."

"Holy shit!" Simon spilled his beer on himself from the astonishment in reaction to what his brother just told him.

"How could you?" He sat blinking rapidly waiting for a reply.

"I...I...wasn't thinking, more over I took her virginity." Veronica had yet to tell him that she was not a virgin and so he was still under the assumption that she was.

"Wow." Simon couldn't think of an intelligent response so he just let what he was thinking come out.

"Man, I tell you it was great, but I was wrong, and now I'm so in to her that I can't turn back."

"I'd say. I really don't know what to tell you but you had better come up with something before dad hears about all of this from someone else." Al knew his brother was right. He was sure that only a few knew about him and Veronica if any outside Simon, but he was even more certain that if he didn't tell his father about Samantha and her pregnancy, Simon Sr. was sure to hear one way or another and he didn't want that kind of news coming from anyone else.

"Yeah, I don't think dad is going to have a pleasant reaction to all of this."

"I think that is putting it mildly, little brother." Simon said as he rose from his seat before he went into the rest room to clean the beer stain from his shirt.

106

Chapter Thirteen

Simon Carter Sr. looked as if he were about to have a heart attack. His face had turned crimson red, his eyes were bloodshot, and numerous veins started bulging from various spots around his face and neck.

"Son," He said trying to calm his frayed nerves. "What do you mean Samantha is with child?"

"Like I said, she's about five months and says that it's mine."

"I can't believe this, you knocked her up. Where was your head? Wait, I know, buried between her fucking legs, right?" Simon's anger was fever pitch. Al was worried that his father's blood pressure had risen to an unknown level.

"Dad calm down, these things happen to consenting adults and like it or not that is what I am, an adult. I'll handle this."

"You're damned right you'll handle this. You are going to do the right thing and marry Sam. I will not have any bastard grandchildren." Al was too astonished at the words his father had spoken to get angry, but once the initial feeling wore off Al was to his feet and inches away from Simon's face.

"Let's get a couple of things clear, I don't give a damn what you will not have because it's not your child, your responsibility, or your life. Secondly I don't nor do I have any intentions on having a relationship beyond our child with Samantha Riley. Now that we are clear, I have more to tell you father." Simon had never seen his son so upset and it unsettled him.

"What more do you have to tell son?" Simon asked calmly.

"I am in a semi-relationship with Veronica Parker?"

"From the restaurant?" Al nodded his response and chanced a furtive glance at the elder man. "What do you mean a 'semi-relationship'?"

"I mean we've been intimate and there are other things going on, but I don't think you need all the details, I'll spare you that much."

"Gee, thanks." Simon said sarcastically. Simon had calmed a great deal due to his son's assertiveness and forthrightness just a few moments prior. He reached for the bottle of aged Brandy sitting on his study desk tray, but changed his mind after seeing the look of concern mar his son's face.

"I don't think that one glass is such a bad thing considering the circumstances, son." Simon Sr. offered in argument for his defense. Al would not have it. Al grabbed the bottle from his father and moved it to the cabinet on the other side of the room. Al went into the small refrigerator and removed a bottle of sparkling water. He grabbed a glass and placed a slice of lemon in it and placed the items before his father. Simon Sr. gave his son a look of disapproval but took the proffered items anyway.

"God what I wouldn't give to have one of your grandmothers caipirinha's, there's nothing like them." Simon Sr. was referring to Al's maternal grandmother, Flavia. She was known in her hometown of Ouro Puerto for the lime, sugar, and alcohol concoction. Al sympathized with his father's desire to drown his worries in the drink indigenous to Brazil, but he also knew that doing so would not be a wise choice for his father and his bad health. Simon Sr's blood pressure was very high and his cholesterol wasn't looking very well either. Mariana and his physician agreed that a better diet, some time off work, and proper rest would do him some good.

"Does Ms. Parker know about Sam's pregnancy?"

"Yeah, she was seating Sam and her date when I showed up and Sam told anyone within earshot that she was carrying my child.' Al hadn't seen Veronica in about two weeks since he left her apartment. He wasn't sure if she was avoiding him, if he was avoiding her, or if they were both avoiding each other. No matter who was avoiding who, because of this Al hadn't seen that Veronica's weight had ballooned.

"What are you going to do son?" Simon's question startled Al. Al was used to his father ordering his actions for him. Because of this it took Al a few minutes before he cleared his throat and spoke.

"I intend on having joint or full custody of my child. I also intend on moving forward with Veronica. I wasn't so sure about doing so before, but now I am."

"How can you be so sure son?"

"Because I'm in love with her dad." Without another word being said Al had convinced his father that he was truly and undoubtedly in love with the woman he said he was. What Simon Sr. was worried about was if Veronica felt the same for his son.

****

"Well hello Ms. Parker. I haven't seen you in a while. How are you?"

"I'm fine Isabel and you?"

"Couldn't be better, are you here to see Mr. Carter?"

"Depends on which Mr. Carter you refer to Isabel, there are quite a few around here." Veronica stated in humor to the older woman. She was trying to stall for time. She knew full well that Al had requested that she meet him for lunch at his office. They had been very successful at avoiding each other for the past few weeks. Veronica did so because she'd told him the mourning after he spent the night at her place that she could not see him in that capacity anymore, not that they were seeing each other that way, but she felt better if she drew lines in the sand before things got out of control.

Al's response was not at all what she expected. "Fine, Veronica. If this is what you want I will grant it for you. For now, but please understand that we will be together. I can't do too much right now as far as argument goes. I have things in my life I need to clear up and I don't want to impose on you with those issues."

Veronica was set for an argument but got none and had to admit to herself that she was actually disappointed that she didn't. She was almost hoping that Al would convince her that they could be together and everything would work out for them. She was almost set to tell him of her pregnancy until she got his response to her feelings.

Standing at Isabel's desk she knew she had no choice but to tell him. It was obvious that she'd gained weight and she had begun to show. Amazingly, all of her extra weight had gone directly to her midsection, aiding in the guessing of her condition. For her size, she had a comparatively small waist, so she was either absurdly bloated or she was pregnant. The knowing look on Isabel's face told her that the time for game playing was over and she had to step up and be a woman.

"Go right in, Al's expecting you."

"Thanks, I'll see you later."

"Yes you will, Veronica." Isabel's normal pleasant sweet sounding voice was gone and her face held a questioning look as Veronica passed her desk and placed her hand on the knob to the entry to Al's office. Veronica looked back at Isabel who gave her a reassuring nod before Veronica twisted her hand and entered Al's office.

The beginning of March found the city with a massive snowstorm and it was all but shut down. But nonetheless, Pingcho, the deliveryman from the Chinese restaurant, mounted his bike to make a delivery. Al watched as the man with limited English tried to peddle through the heavy snow and icy ground from his office window. He knew Veronica was in the office and watching him but refused to turn to look at her. He was tired of always coming to her and would not do it another time.

"Al, you wanted to see me?" Al smiled and turned his body more towards the window he didn't want to chance her seeing him smirk. Small step, but it'll do. He thought to himself.

Veronica was humbling herself and it was hard for her, however both she and Al felt it was time she did. She figured that she had to have a healthy helping of humility before she walked in the office because the circumstances had changed and she could no longer make demands of him. Veronica had been unfair to the man with his back to her. She had pushed him away after misleading him to think that they had gotten closer, she had neglected to correct him in his assumptions about her past, and more unforgivable she'd hidden the fact that she was carrying his child from him. Her doctor had determined that she was just into her second trimester and set her due date for September.

"Al?" Veronica wasn't sure he'd heard her and called his name to get his attention.

"I heard you Veronica." He confirmed. He turned slowly in her direction and instantly noticed her physical change. Color left his natural tanned skin and he reached for something to stable him self. The reality of it all hit him like a bulldozer.

"You're expecting?" He knew that the question was asinine, the very least a statement of the obvious, but couldn't help voicing his thoughts.

"Si Alejandro, estoy embarasada." Veronica confirmed in Spanish.

"Why didn't you tell me? And before you speak make sure it's a good excuse, por favor." The seething tone of his voice caused Veronica to take a few steps back until her back was flush against the door. She felt trapped and cornered but she had no other choice than to face the music. It was the bed she'd made of bad choices and the time had come for her to sleep in it.

"I didn't know how to tell you."

"What the hell do you mean you didn't know how?" Veronica tried to move further back but the door stood in her way. She was truly frightened as Al stalked towards her and pinned her against the solid wood barrier. Al stood so close to Veronica that it bordered on erotic. Her swollen breasts pressed into his hard muscled body and it took all she could muster not to touch him.

Al sensed that Veronica was scared of him and at that particular moment he really didn't care, if he was being honest with him self he was actually getting some pleasure out of it. She had blatantly with held pertinent information from him all the while dangling him on an emotional string. She deserved a lot more than to feel threatened by him, but he was not Veronica nor was he her judge. Al was beyond the point of angry but somewhere in the recesses of his fury was compassion and understanding for Veronica.

"Could you give me just a little space please?" Veronica's moment of fright was smoothly replaced by indignation. Al was amazed at how quickly she recuperated. He was even more frustrated at how quickly she could turn a situation to her favor. He was determined not to give her an inch of reprieve.

"Not until you tell me what the hell is going on!" His eyes had darkened and looked black in color.

"You already know what's going on Alejandro!" Her retaliation seemed futile at best. "I am pregnant and it is your child."

"How long have you known Veronica?" His voice had dropped to a husky whisper that was so heated it could boil water.

"Since Christmas."

"And you didn't tell me?"

"No, I didn't and before we go around in circles, I already told you that I didn't know how to tell you about it."

"Didn't know how or didn't want to?" The question hung in the air like a helium balloon, fat, bloated, and ready to pop. "I didn't know how. I was going to tell you but then you got the news of your other child, and I just felt the timing wasn't right."

Al backed away from Veronica. His head was spinning and he felt like the world had turned up side down. He had just begun to come to terms with the situation he was in with Samantha only to have Veronica throw another stone his way.

"Well I guess you didn't sleep with me to get the job now did you?" Al regretted his words the instant they left his mouth and wished that Veronica had slapped him before he spoke instead of after. As it stood he probably deserved more than her hand across his face but he figured an eye for an eye.

Rubbing the spot where her hand made loud contact with his face Al turned from Veronica and walked over to his desk and picked up his phone. "Bel, could you cancel the rest of my appointments and tell my brother that I'm leaving the office for the day." Al looked across the room at Veronica; she was still standing against the door like it was offering her some sort of solace. "Call over to Four Corners and tell them that Miss Parker will not be returning for the remainder of the afternoon either." There was a pause as Al listened to Isabel's comments then he gave her his thanks and hung up the receiver.

"Let's go." Al commanded as he went to the coat hanger and grabbed his down coat. Al knew that the weather was expected to be bad and had not wanted to wait for the train that day and decided to drive into work. He was thankful for his decision because he could take Veronica back to his place to talk.

"I'm not going any where with you!" Veronica crossed her arms. Her eyes had steeled over with pure hatred aimed at Al.

"Yes you are, we need to talk and I'm not about to do that here."

"That's funny you seem to do a lot of inappropriate things here why not add this to your list?" Veronica was aching to verbally insult him in the manner he had insulted her but she knew that the chances of that happening were slim to none.

"You're right, but I'm trying to make amends for my behavior."

****

Al had a new model car with plush leather interior and wood grain molding. He had a Latin music CD playing in the changer. He was singing along with the man in the song. The lyrics were about love and honor and how the woman he'd given those things to abused them.

"You can find something else to listen to if you don't want to hear this. The CD book is under your seat." Veronica was grateful for his offer; she wasn't in the mood to hear about some man wronged by a woman in matters of the heart.

When Veronica opened the CD organizer she was surprised to find a wide array of selections. The music was neatly organized by genre he had soul, rock, funk, Latin, R&B, and Classical. Veronica decided to listen to one of the R&B albums. She put in a newer artist that she liked and skipped to one of her favorite songs.

The song played and commanded Al and Veronica's full attention. The sultry voice pumping out the speakers spoke of how her and her lover could be worlds apart and would always be connected to one another in their hearts. By the song's end Veronica was in tears and could careless if Al saw her cry. In fact she wanted him to see the agony she was in.

"I want you to move in with me Veronica." Al said without taking his eyes off the tumultuous snow covered road. He had wanted to offer her a traditional courting but he didn't want her away from him and her moving in with him seemed the logical solution.

"What?" Veronica asked between sobs.

"I want you to move in with me. I think it would be best for you and the baby." Al was almost as shocked as Veronica at the proposition he'd made.

"You want me to move in with you and then what Al? I'm going to share a room with your other woman? I can't believe that you even suggested such a thing." Veronica was recovering from her crying bout and her mind had begun to clear. They rode in silence for the remainder of the trip to his apartment. The only sound around them was the singer's voice crooning about how she wouldn't complain about life's troubles if the love of her life would return.

Veronica hadn't realized that Al lived as close to her home as he did. He'd told her that it wasn't a far walk but she didn't know that his residence was in fact just a ten-minute walk from her apartment building.

Once inside Veronica shed her winter coverings and asked Al where the bathroom was. She had begun to fit a cliché thought of pregnant women; she had to go to the bathroom regularly. He directed her to the one inside his bedroom but she flatly refused and went to the one in the hall.

Al's apartment was a sprawling layout. It had three bedrooms, two full bathrooms, and a garden terrace area that he shared with the other two apartments on his floor. The hard wood floors and crown molding were just a small indication of the wealth seeping from the residence. The bathroom in the hall was twice the size of her own bathroom, and the kitchen was a chef's dream.

Once she returned to the living room Veronica found Al standing by the French doors that lead to the terrace staring at the falling snow.

"We need to talk about this Veronica. We can't go back and forth on this." She knew he was right but she couldn't help resisting the obvious.

"I don't think we have much to talk about. I have no problem raising this child on my own and I certainly don't mind him or her not knowing who their father is."

"How can you say such a thing when less than twenty minutes ago you were crying in my car?"

"I can say it with ease. You have a lot of shit going on in your life and I can't be a part of that, I won't subject my self or my child to that." Veronica had taken a seat on his sage green leather recliner. The softness of the chair was dangerously close to lulling Veronica to sleep. She had not been able to sleep comfortably for weeks. Through heavy lids and a loud yawn Veronica said, "I can't do that, Al. What would we do? Live together, date, or raise your illegitimate seed in the perfect lie?"

"First and foremost understand that the child you carry is not your child nor my 'seed' as you put it, that child is ours." Veronica looked as if she was about to interrupt him but he held up his hand to silence her retort then continued. "Yes it's true Samantha's pregnancy came as a surprise but I didn't plan it, we used protection, but I don't want to be with Samantha I want to be with you."

"I don't know that I can believe that you had the sense to protect Samantha because you didn't with me." Veronica said tartly through another yawn.

"I know I didn't protect you and I'm sorry, but I also know that she is way more experienced than you. She had other partners than me and to be brutally honest, she was just something to do. I took your virginity for crying out loud, in my office of all places..." It was Veronica's turn to placate Al. She knew that the topic of her virtue would come up again sooner or later. She was hoping for never but knew that was wishful thinking.

"I wasn't a virgin when you slept with me Al; as a matter of fact I'd had two other partners before you." Al looked at her confused then suddenly the creases in his forehead disappeared and Al had a look of understanding on his face. He turned his body so that he was fully facing her and crossed his arms over his massive chest. "Tell me what happened." The statement came out as an order but Veronica understood why. Al sensed her bitterness when she spoke of her previous partners and wanted to know what happened to her when she was much younger.

"I was going out with a guy when I was fifteen and..."

"What guy? And why were you going out with him at such a young age?"

"Just a guy, no need to go into details about him, he doesn't matter anymore." Veronica got a far off look in her eye before she continued to talk. "Don't interrupt again, this is hard enough for me to talk about, okay?"

"Sorry, I won't do it again. Please continue."

"Anyway I was seeing him and we were getting along pretty well and then one day I was at his and his brother's apartment." Veronica paused to get her composure. She hadn't discussed the incident with anyone outside of Renee, Nick, and just recently her mother. Veronica saw the look on Al's face and knew that their had been a question burning inside him that he could hardly contain. She decided to let him speak. "What?" She asked.

"How old was he?"

"Twenty." She responded while averting her eyes.

"Go on." Al wanted to ask what she was doing with some one that much older than she but refrained from doing so.

"I was over at his place and we went to his room. We had sex and then he left the room and told me to stay put." Veronica took a gulp of air. "I thought he was coming back into the room when I saw the door open but it wasn't him, it was his brother Marc." Veronica stopped to look at Al; she didn't see the disgust that she'd expected only caring and understanding. "Marc came in the room and gave me this spill on how we were family and family shares everything. Then he...he said that I should give him what I gave his brother. I didn't want to do it but I was scared." Veronica started to cry but felt she had to get the rest of the story out. By this time Al was sitting on the arm of the recliner and was holding Veronica by the shoulders and placed a kiss atop her head in silent urge for her to finish.

"He got on top of me and made me have sex with him, he said I wanted it but I didn't. I didn't want any of it. I didn't want to sleep with him. I didn't want to get pregnant. I didn't want to get rid of the baby, I didn't want to. I swear I didn't." Veronica began to cry uncontrollably. Al lifted her out of the chair and escorted her into his bedroom. He removed her shoes and swung her legs onto the bed. Her crying had yet to cease and it was one that she didn't mind the overflow of emotion.

Veronica had years of frustration, shame, and embarrassment bottled up inside of her. No one had ever accused her of leading Justin and his brother to believe that they could violate her with such ease yet they had. No one had told Veronica that she should not be ashamed of what happened to her, yet she was. No one had to convince Al to want to go out and find the men responsible for harming Veronica and cause them slow and painful bodily harm, yet he did.

Veronica cried herself into slumber in Al's arms. Al watched as Veronica slept soundly in his arms for a while before the rumble in his stomach caused him to leave the bedroom and find nourishment. As soon as Al closed his bedroom door behind him he heard the chirp sound of Veronica's cell phone and made his way to her shoulder bag to retrieve it. He didn't think twice about answering it seeing how he didn't want to disturb Veronica's sleep.

"Hello." His voice held a slight baritone timber that some would say was too deep for him, while others felt that it was alluring and sexy.

"Who is this? Where's my daughter?" Tammy Parker's worried voice came through the earpiece. Tammy was alarmed when she'd gone to her daughter's job to find out that she'd unexpectedly left for the remainder of the day.

"This is Alejandro Carter and your daughter is sleeping Mrs. Parker."

"It's Ms. Parker and what is she doing with you?" Al couldn't mistake the hostility in Veronica's mother's voice.

"She came to my office for lunch and I was surprised to find that she was with child, my child to be exact." Al was determined not to let the severity of the situation and Tammy's inquiry upset him. He was to be a father two times over in the next few months and he was not going to lose Veronica and what he wanted with her to circumstance and a mother's bad attitude.

"She told you?" Tammy asked breaking into his thoughts.

"Not exactly, I could see her weight gain and assumed that it was due to one thing." Al sat on the ottoman near his right leg.

"She hasn't gained that much weight, she's hardly any different than the last time you saw each other."

"However small the change, I would notice it on Veronica." Al said smugly.

"You know, I don't really like your tone and I certainly don't like my daughter being there with you, alone."

"I'm sorry you feel that way, but to be honest it's really none of your concern." Al almost regretted the manner in which he addressed Tammy Parker, but then again she started the minor confrontation.

"Like hell it isn't my concern. In case you didn't know it, Veronica is my daughter and that is my grandchild that she happens to be carrying. So if you think that you can speak to me any ole kind of way, you are so mistaken." Al had a fleeting thought of disconnecting the call and turning off Veronica's cell phone, however he knew once Veronica found out he'd be the one suffering.

Taking a deep breath Al spoke "You're right Ms. Parker and I'm sorry for my earlier disposition, it's just that all of this is rather overwhelming for me."

"Call me Tammy, Alejandro. You should have nothing to feel overwhelmed about. You and Ronnie are adults who made adult decisions and now the both of you, together, have to deal with the consequences."

"Easier said than done." Al countered sarcastically. The sound of helplessness in his voice alarmed Tammy.

She'd not thought of Al as someone who backed down from a challenge much less as someone who resigned to difficult situations. She was beginning to wonder if her daughter had fallen for someone not strong enough to support Veronica and her child.

Tammy was not one to think her child incompetent or even needy. But she did however know that she had faced many adversities by herself because that was how she had wanted things. This situation was not one that Veronica could do by herself and no one was aware of this more than Tammy. She'd raised her daughter on her own without the help and support of family or friends until Nick came along and it was hard.

Tammy had to endure many distasteful comments, stares, and outright rudeness for having a child out of wedlock and as a teen. Although times had changed many views about unwed mothers remained the same. Veronica was a very strong and willful young woman, but she also lacked knowledge about many worldly things and she was going to need someone to be there for her, mentally, physically, and emotionally. Tammy had reservations if Alejandro Carter would be strong enough to be able to handle all the things Veronica was going to throw his way.

"That is very true, but resignation will not do. Ronnie is in an outstanding predicament, as well as your self. You will have to be strong for the both of you. She may come off as this strong independent woman who neither needs nor wants anyone to help her with anything, but she's not. She is going to need you to support her, this is going to be hard for the both of you, and for yours, Ronnie's, and the baby's sake you have to be strong and make this work."

"I know, most people don't admit their weaknesses but I broadcast mine, and I have a weakness for your daughter. I also can't seem to get my life together. I don't know if you are aware of this but Veronica is not the only woman who carries a child of mine. I..." Tammy did not want any explanations about his and Samantha's child. She cut him off before he continued in his statement. "Al please;

as I said before you and Ronnie are adults and so I cannot and will not be a sounding board for any guilt that you hold. As long as my daughter is happy and you can care for her in a manner that she deserves, then that is all I require of you, understood?" Al was silent for an uncomfortable period of time.

"I understand, and I'll try my best to fulfill your wishes."

"Don't worry about trying to do anything for me, you make sure that your efforts are not wasted and do not let my daughter run over you. She has this uncanny ability to push people away and they don't realize it until it's too late." Al wanted Tammy to expand the meaning of her words but he thought better of trying to get the straight talking woman to bull's eye him with her words. He knew what Tammy meant, Veronica handled her problems and those involved with her problems by dealing with them on an individual basis. She pushed everyone around her away and then used some sort of sentimental excuse as her reasoning.

"I am coming there when I get off work, tell me your address." Tammy ordered. Al didn't want Veronica's mother to come to his home but knew that he didn't have much in the area of options of staving her off. Al rattled off his address and told Tammy that he would inform Veronica of her arrival.

Chapter Fourteen

No sign of snow outside was the pleasant view from the window of the moving train. All Veronica could see was the briskly passing scenery, cows, horses, trucks with leisurely drivers waiting for the cross roads signs to rise and let them pass. Pulling her attention away from the window she could see an elderly couple approaching the seats across from her. They were so in love, she in her golden dress looking regal and him in all black looking as if he had been a beacon of strength for her for many years and more to come.

The elderly woman was African-American and the man was Caucasian, they looked as if they were almost one in the same person. They spoke to each other in complete silence. The look of love for one another radiated a glow from them. So bright their smiles were, so happy they were. One man, one woman, with outside beauty surrounding them.

Then the train went into a tunnel and it became dark and when it came out on the other side and light returned and the couple was gone. Sitting in their place sat Al and Samantha holding their baby. The sight mesmerized Veronica. She tried to say something but no sound came out as she opened her mouth. She tried to move out of her seat, she wanted to get Al's attention, tell him how she felt but Justin and Marc stood in her way.

Tears now filled her eyes and Veronica couldn't control the emotional spilling. Marc and Justin stood blocking her way and then with out warning Veronica woke from her dream. She wasn't on a train, the old couple didn't exist,

Samantha and Al weren't doting over their child, but Veronica was most definitely hurting from the vision.

The hall light crept into the room as Al opened the door and walked in the room.

"What's wrong Veronica?" He'd heard her yell out in mortified pain and then start crying, the noise caused him to drop the bowl of pasta he'd prepared on the floor and go running in the direction of his room just seconds before.

Veronica still stuck in a place somewhere between consciousnesses and deep sleep heard Al's voice and wailed even louder. Al knelt beside his bed and turned on the lamp so that he could see her. Once the soft light flooded the room he realized that she wasn't fully awake.

"Ronnie, baby wake up, it's a nightmare. Baby wake up!" Veronica's eyes fluttered open and she became aware of her surroundings and that the train ride was a dream never to come true.

It was dark out side and another snowfall had begun and large white flakes settled outside the bedroom window on the outer ledge. Veronica concentrated on Mother Nature's volatile yet stunning work until she was able to speak.

"I was on this train. And there was this older couple they were so in love. Then it got dark and when the light came back they were gone and then...then...you were there." More tears cut off Veronica's words.

"You don't have to talk about it. It was a nightmare. Not real. I am right here with you okay." He was pleading. Al wanted to take all of Veronica's pain and burn it in a furnace so that she would never hurt again.

Al knew that he hadn't caused Marc and Justin to violate Veronica and that he had no control over the suffering she'd experienced before they met, however it didn't dull the guilt he felt at seeing her in pain.

He knelt on the floor for a long time stroking Veronica's face, trying to smooth her pain away. Veronica hated that she'd gotten so emotional over the past weeks. Prior to her getting pregnant she could hold her own or at least she could do a better job of it than what she'd been doing. It seemed as if once she became pregnant she couldn't turn off the spigots of tears.

The last thing she felt that she needed was someone to feel sorry for her and more importantly for Al to feel sorry for her. She'd come to the conclusion that him feeling sorry for her lead him to say and do things that he probably wouldn't normally have, things like asking her to live with him. Had she not slept with him and completely thrown rational thinking out the door, they would not be in the predicament that they found themselves. That with standing, she was not going to let his conscience cause him to make any more bad decisions.

"Al, I really appreciate your offer, and I understand that you were trying to do the right thing but I can't possibly move in with you." She'd gained most of her composure and had finally gotten her self together enough to speak. She continued, "I can't let you ruin your life and everything that you've worked for on my account. If you want I can make this all go away?"

Al sat blinking rapidly at Veronica. Did she just say what I think she just said? He wasn't totally sure of what Veronica meant by 'make this all go away', but he did know that he didn't like what he was hearing.

"What do you mean, Veronica?" He wasn't a man to make speculations and a lot of assumptions so she would have to spell everything out to him.

"I mean that I could maybe get rid of it, or maybe re-sign my position so that no one would know. There's no need for office gossip to get fierce. You don't owe me anything." Disbelief didn't, nor couldn't describe what he was feeling. Veronica had the gall to sit in his home, in his face and actually present the idea of aborting a child, namely his child, as if it that were an option. To add fuel to the fire she even went so far as to suggest that she simply go away so that he wouldn't suffer.

"Are you out of your goddamn mind!?" Al didn't recognize his own voice through the rage billowing from him. "How dare you even insinuate that I am that kind of man, or that you are that kind of woman for that matter?"

Veronica lay on her side with her head propped on her hand. She was surprised that she had remained as calm as she was. On any other occasion she would not accept anyone raising a voice at her, but she was willing to make an exception for Al. She had just told him that he was free of obligation from her and while his attempt at anger showing offense was notable, Veronica thought that her suggestion was very generous.

"I'm not insinuating an abortion, I won't do that again. I was thinking of placing the child up for adoption. Al, I know that you have a lot to deal with right now and these problems aren't that easy to fix or even just ignore, and they're not going to just disappear."

"Isn't that what you just offered to do, go away?" Al was hissing but Veronica decided to ignore his tone and continue.

"In a way, yes, I don't want to inconvenience your life. I can go away, maybe move to Florida with my grandparents." Veronica's calm demeanor was slowly fading, the more she spoke the more her hurt and self-pity grew. She didn't want to go away but she also felt there was no future for her and Al. They came from two different worlds and didn't share common goals in life. A child was not in the plans for them, hell sleeping with her employer was definitely not in the plans for Veronica, but it happened, and she was willing to let Al concede his responsibility.

Al wanted to grab Veronica by her shoulders and shake her till she got some sense in her beautiful head. He'd heard of women loosing their wits during pregnancy but he couldn't believe that Veronica had gone plain stupid.

"Ronnie I'm trying to be calm here, but if you think for one minute that I'm going to let you sit here and talk to me like this you're crazy." Al paused to gather his thoughts. He wanted to convey his feeling for Veronica to her properly and without overwhelming her. "I told you before that I care for you deeply and I do not want to be with Samantha. I do however want to be a part of her and my child's life. I also want you to be a part of my life. I really don't know what I'm offering but I know that I don't want to be away from you."

Veronica could tell that Al was sincere in his words but she couldn't help having her reservations. The sound of the intercom broke into Veronica's thoughts and made her jump in surprise.

"Are you expecting someone?" Veronica questioned. Her suspicious tone was not lost on Al but he decided not to pursue the subject.

"Yes, we are expecting someone." He said emphasizing the word we. "That should be your mother." He said and rose off the floor. Straightening his pants he walked out of the room and called back to a dumbfounded Veronica. "Ronnie your mother is on her way up and dinner is almost done, I suggest you go get cleaned up so we all can eat."

****

The pasta and grilled salmon that Al prepared was absolutely wonderful, however Veronica didn't have much of an appetite and barely finished half her plate.

Her mother and Al discussed her life and future as if she weren't in the room. She was compelled to interrupt their chatter but she couldn't stand to tear away her mother's happiness of becoming a grandmother. Tammy went on and on how she was so pleased that Ronnie was pregnant, despite the circumstances. Her reserve faltered when Tammy agreed with Al's thinking and suggested that maybe Veronica should consider moving in with him. At first Veronica wasn't positive she'd heard her mother correctly but when her mother repeated the statement Veronica was sure that she had not all of a sudden become hard of hearing.

Despite her nap Veronica felt drained and had no energy to argue with her mother or Al so she decided to take up battle with the both of them on separate occasions, she didn't want them to gang up on her at that particular moment.

Tammy had taken the liberty to pick up a few items for Veronica on her way to Al's condo. Veronica took the notion as Tammy's way of letting Veronica know that she felt that her daughter should stay at Al's at least for a few days. Normally Veronica wouldn't have made such an assumption but her mother had packed a suitcase for her. Subtlety was not a strong point for Tammy Parker.

Veronica sat silently and listened while her mother all but offered Veronica's hand in marriage to Al. Veronica was too pissed off to be amazed at how well Tammy and Al got along. Knowing Tammy all too well, Veronica suspected that this was not the first time the two had talked, when they had the opportunity to do so was beyond Veronica at that moment.

"Please excuse me; I would like to lie down." Veronica rose from her seat to two sets of worried and concerned eyes.

"Are you feeling okay?" Al asked in Spanish.

"Si, I am fine, Alejandro." Al knew that she wasn't telling him and her mother the truth; he'd learned in a very short time that she only called him Alejandro when she was peeved at him.

"What's the matter, Ronnie?" Tammy inquired.

"Why don't you and Alejandro figure it out together, seems the two of you have no problem discussing my life without my participation. Just keep it going." Tammy and Al gave each other confused looks. They were not sure where Veronica's latest mood swing had come from.

Veronica went to the hall cloak closet and grabbed her coat and goulashes then started to put them on.

"What do you think you're doing?" Al asked.

"I'm leaving. I am going back to my place?"

"No you're not. Now take your coat off."

"Since when did you start ordering me around? I have you to know I took care of myself before I met you and I'm sure that I'll continue to do so."

"I have every right if I feel that the health of my child and the woman carrying said child is at stake."

"I truly understand your concern, Mr. Carter, but as I said I can handle myself."

"Callate!" Tammy yelled at the both of them to stop the argument. Tammy had to pull together all of her strength to keep her smile at bay. Never in her life had she known her daughter to get so worked up over a man.

"Can't the two of you talk to one another with out arguing? You weren't fighting and bickering when you two made this baby, I suggest that you refer to what it was that brought you all together in the first place and make this thing work."

Al helped Veronica out of her coat and placed it back into the closet. Veronica wanted desperately to find a place and hide but the open floor plan of Al's condo betrayed her need for reprieve. Making eye contact with her more than practical mother was not an option for Veronica. Looking Tammy in the eye would just confirm her thoughts; she was behaving like a spoiled child. A brat would be a more appropriate term but she would not go so far as to call herself that.

Veronica wasn't exactly sure why she kept trying to pull away from Al, she just kept doing it. She'd start an argument just so she wouldn't have to have civil conversation with him. Underneath she knew it was very silly and childish but she felt safer when she did. Never in her life had she felt so strongly connected to another person outside her family and she didn't know how to handle that feeling. On top of that she had to deal with her feelings towards Samantha and the child fathered by Al that she carried.

"It seems so simple to you, but I'm the one who has to deal with all of this."

"Not by your self, Ronnie." Al interjected.

"Yes, by my self, Al. Neither of you can feel for me, I have to deal with that internally, by my self. However I don't have to go at it alone." Veronica paused and finally made eye contact with her mother. "Al my mom is right. We have to at least be civil with one another and if you're willing to forgive my behavior I'm willing to give a shot at being friends." It wasn't exactly what Al wanted but he was willing to give Veronica what she asked for.

He wanted Veronica to concede to his request and move in with him but he knew he was reaching really far. He had to make Veronica realize he needed her; that he felt incomplete when she wasn't near, that he sat up at night because he couldn't handle the dreams of her. He needed Veronica to know how much he cared for her, how much he wanted and needed her in his life. Sitting across his living room from the woman who made him whole Al decided he would not rest until she was his, and only his.

She didn't know it but Veronica's apology to Al made him very happy. To him she was taking steps at compromise and her own personal growth. He didn't want to break her spirit, which was one of her most attractive assets; he simply wanted her to be at peace with herself.

"That's not good enough Ronnie." Tammy's voice of reason chimed in.

"Ms. Parker, it's okay. It's enough for me." Al was set to defend Veronica when Tammy put an end to his intentions.

"It is not okay, Alejandro. And you of all people should know that. Veronica this is the father of your child and while being friends would have been an option for you before you got into all of this, it's a little late for that."

"Ma, I am not going to marry the man just because I am with his child!" Al could see that the two women were at the beginning of a heated discussion and wanted to stop it, but he couldn't bring himself to do so. The whole scene was like a very bad car wreck, brutal, unsightly, and he couldn't tear his eyes away from the sight of it.

"I didn't say you had to marry him but you will not play with his emotions or your own. Just a few weeks ago you sat at the diner and spilled your guts about how you felt about Al and how you didn't know what to do, well God has given you the answer and you still want to resist, Why?"

"I don't have to listen to this!"

"Yes you do, and I don't know who you think you're raising your voice, at but I suggest you fix your tone and remember just who you're talking to." Veronica took a deep breath before she spoke. "Listen to me, I have offered Al my promise to be civil and to work with him on this. I can't offer much more than that."

"Can't or won't, Ronnie?" Tammy was not going to let her daughter off easy and everyone present in the room knew it. "I don't know where I failed you to make you so scared of life and all its nuances but you had better get used to a little something called change because it's going to happen every day, and that little fact will never change."

Veronica was against the odds but she was determined not to let her Mother bully her. Because of the obvious love that she carried in her heart for her mother Veronica was prone to do just about anything her mother asked her to do, except this one thing. Veronica had not had much experience with men but the little that she'd had was not pleasant and she couldn't all of a sudden get over that.

Yes, it had been nearly ten years since the incident with Marc and Justin but to Veronica it seemed like yesterday. For one fleeting moment in her life she thought someone cared for her because they chose to, not from legal or genetic obligation. It was obvious that Tammy, Nick, and Renee cared a great deal for her but Veronica couldn't help think that they only cared for her out of some sort of obligation, not because they just cared for her.

That one blemish on Veronica's self esteem had kept her from getting close to any man outside of Nick. In high school she thought that the boys only wanted to talk to her to try to get her to do their assignments for them and after that horrible evening with Marc and Justin she felt all men only wanted to hurt her. Veronica became so determined to succeed that she became practically a hermit while pursuing her degree. If an activity didn't serve the purpose academics and furthering her career, Veronica didn't participate. Veronica believed that she was satisfied with her life and how it worked, but apparently everyone else around her had a different view.

Chapter Fifteen

The ringing phone had awakened Veronica out of her slumber. She wasn't sure how long she had been asleep or where she was for that matter but she picked up the receiver to the loud and annoying instrument. By the time she had effectively placed the phone near her ear she could hear that a conversation was already taking place.

"You can't be serious, Al. I mean let's be real about all of this. You can't be at all serious about that girl."

"Sam I can't believe that you called me to talk about my relationship with Veronica." Veronica recognized the voices belonging to Al and Samantha and suddenly became fully aware of her where abouts, she was asleep in Al's master bedroom, in his bed.

How could she have forgotten what had transpired just two days before? After three weeks of intensive pleading and arguing and a chance robbery at knife point, Veronica agreed to move in with Al. Tammy, Renee, and Nick had all agreed that Veronica should stay with Al, but Veronica was not so willing to concede to the suggestion, but once she was accosted by an individual wielding a deadly weapon her perspective changed and she went straight to Al's apartment.

It was just after midnight that evening when Veronica got off work, George had called to inform her that he was very ill and would not be able to work. He suggested that she call in one of the assistants or have someone stay over to cover the evening but Veronica said that she could handle it and asked him not to worry. It was a Wednesday so the restaurant wasn't expected to be too busy after the after work crowd cleared. More people had come in than expected, the weather had turned out to be very pleasant for early April so the people of Cleveland got out to enjoy it.

Four Corners closed at ten-thirty Sunday thru Thursday but so many people kept coming in it stayed open until eleven that night. Veronica made it out of the restaurant just in time to catch the last train to her neighborhood. She was actually relieved because she didn't have enough money for a cab. Normally that wouldn't be a problem because she could bum a ride from someone but she had told everyone that she was going to catch a cab so no one would have to come get her at such a late hour.

Only she and three other people were on the train ride home including the operator. A very athletic man had gotten off two stops before hers and that left Veronica and a seedy looking derelict of a man as passengers. When the operator announced her stop Veronica stood and so did the mangy looking man. She was a little leery but figured the man wouldn't bother her.

Veronica descended the steps off the train and the man followed. She turned one way and he turned the other. She let out a breath of relief. She hadn't realized how nervous she was until she was away from the man. Not more than a few seconds after she began her journey towards her apartment building the man appeared from what seemed like nowhere asking Veronica for a light for a cigarette.

"I'm sorry but I don't smoke." Veronica responded. The forecast for the day had been for a storm to come, but up until that point it was just overcast. The weather had held up rather well for the whole day. When Veronica tried to move away from her assailant the sky opened and a fierce downpour began.

"I'm sorry." Veronica repeated and tried to turn to leave but the scummy man grabbed her by the arm and would not release her even after Veronica demanded that he do so. Instinct kicked in and Veronica kicked the man in his right shin and broke to run away but the man caught her by the leg. Veronica slipped and fell into a muddy puddle but she didn't notice, all she wanted to do was get away from the strange man. *Oh god please, I am so sorry for everything that I've ever done. Shit! Why didn't I just get a ride home? Think Veronica! Oh my god he's got a knife!*

Veronica and her assailant scrambled on the ground all the while Veronica attempting to escape and he trying to retain her. Finally the two stopped tousling and the man let his true intentions be known. "Give me yo shit bitch!"

"I don't have anything!" Veronica wasn't lying about her not having any possessions, she opted not to carry a purse that day, she wore no jewelry, and she only had about five dollars on her person.

Veronica didn't know it was coming until it had already happened and she was unable to shield her face from the two quick, hard, closed fist blows that the man had administered directly to her face.

"I said give me yo shit!" Veronica went to reach in her pocket for the five dollars that she had. She was disoriented and the cold combined with the pounding the man delivered to her was making her head spin. She was too dizzy and in the throws of adrenaline to notice that the other three punches landed had gashed her left eye and that she was bleeding profusely.

"Hey what are you doing?!" Veronica thought the voice was an angel but it turned out to be Henry Jones, Mrs. Payton's granddaughter's fiancé. Then another voice came, Veronica's own.

"Help me!" Veronica was barely audible her mouth was swollen and bleeding.

"Shut the hell up!" The crazed man raised his hand to inflict another monumental hit to Veronica's battered face but Henry caught his arm and wrestled the man to the ground. Mrs. Payton ran to Veronica to help her to her feet and escort her away from the scene.

Veronica's assailant escaped Henry's rescue and ran off. Henry ran into the lobby area of Mrs. Payton's building to check on Veronica and his future Grandmother in law.

"Ronnie, are you alright?" The look on his face told Veronica all she needed to know; she looked like how she felt, terrible. It was later that she was told that her bruises were superficial. Henry and Mrs. Payton were returning from a late show at the movie theater when they happened upon the horrible scene. Veronica wanted nothing more than to curl up into a ball and cry but she didn't.

"I'm fine Henry, a little cold and worn but I'm okay."

"We need to get you to the hospital and we should call the police so that you can fill out a report." The last thing Veronica wanted to do was to sit and wait forever in the College Hospital emergency room. While the doctors and care received there was excellent one could bleed to death waiting on medical relief.

"No Henry I'm okay I will call the police but I don't want to go to the hospital." Veronica knew that she was putting up a fight for no reason and at minimum required stitches.

All Veronica wanted to do was get to Al. He made her feel safe and had she allowed him to protect as he wanted to, she wouldn't have been caught in the situation in the first place. Al offered to help her purchase a car or to even take his own, but she'd refused, citing that she'd feel like a kept woman. Veronica had been saving to purchase a new car for herself but with the baby coming she was focusing on getting a larger place and things for her child. Now it all seemed stupid. It wasn't like Al wasn't going to provide for their child, she just couldn't let go of her pride. Veronica just wanted to be with Al, in his arms, surrounded by his loving care. Veronica pleaded and argued with Henry but eventually she got her way and he escorted her to Al's apartment.

The doorman's incessant pounding awoke Al from his sleep. Scrambling out of bed he took a glance at his bedside clock saw that it was extremely late. Like a flash, he knew that something was wrong with Veronica and quickly ran to open his door.

The look on Al's face only showed a fraction of the horror he felt. Veronica's sweet beautiful face was marred beyond his worst nightmare. Her lips were swollen, one eye had a bad bloody gash and the other swollen shut. Veronica was doing everything in her power to keep from crying but her resolve was quickly dissipating and she wanted the doorman and Henry to go away so she could lick her wounds in peace, alone.

"What happened?" Al asked in disbelief.

"Mr. Carter this woman..." The doorman made a motion towards Veronica and made the word 'woman' sound dirty. That was Veronica's undoing and despite the awful pain in her head she began to cry.

"Skip, I suggest that you watch your mouth. This 'woman' happens to be my girlfriend and you are completely out of line."

After Henry introduced himself and told Al what had happened to Veronica he excused himself and entrusted Veronica's care to Al.

"Veronica, I'm taking you to the emergency room. Stay here while I put on some clothes." Veronica wanted to argue but knew that she couldn't and her wounds needed medical attention. She was going to need stitches above her left eye.

Since that incident, at Al and Tammy's insistence, Veronica had taken temporary residence in a spare bedroom in Al's apartment.

****

Al couldn't figure out why Veronica had barely touched her dinner, since she'd entered her second trimester he had noticed a significant increase in her eating habits, so her sitting across from him pushing her food around on the plate was unacceptable.

"Veronica, Que te pasa?"

"Nada"

"Liar!" Al was furious. It seemed that once they took two steps forward Veronica became determined to hurl them ten steps backwards. It had been just seven days since her attack and Veronica had yet to step foot outside the apartment unless absolutely necessary and understandably so.

A week was hardly enough time for her wounds to heal, emotionally and physically, however; the swelling had subsided and the bruises were healing nicely. Earlier that day Veronica agreed to Al's insistence that she take a medical leave of absence. Her OB/GYN was genuinely concerned about the toll her job stress and the attack was having on her and the baby. Her blood pressure had begun to fluctuate from abnormally low to dangerously high.

There was no way of convincing any one, including herself, that she was fine to return to work. However Veronica's reluctance to venture outside was not the source of her melancholy mood and Al was not happy with the woman who claimed his heart.

"Why can't you just leave me alone? Do I go around bothering you all the time? No I don't. I leave you be, I don't ask questions, I don't pry, I don't ask where you are going or whom you speak to. Why can't you do the same for me?" Veronica's eyes glistened from unshed tears. *God I hate this. I try to stay strong and all I do is cry. What am I going to do? I can't keep this up much longer.*

Al could tell that Veronica was in a lot of pain and obviously worn out from whatever was on her mind but he refused to relent. If he was the cause of her misery he wanted to know how to rectify the situation.

"Quit yelling at me and tell me what's really bothering you Ronnie."

"Do you still love her?" The words escaped Veronica so fast the she hadn't realized she said them until her hand flew to cover her mouth.

"At last the truth comes out." Al placed his fork on the half eaten plate of food in front of him and pushed the plate away. The excellent meal of pork chops and rice that Veronica had prepared was no longer of interest to him. "Tell me something, does it really matter what answer I give you? You won't believe me either way." The two combatants stared at one another inaudibly for a long while. Veronica calculating her response or if a response was her best move and Al silently fuming at himself for falling so hard for a woman who specialized in getting under his skin.

"Al, I'm sor-"

"Damn it Ronnie, I don't want you to apologize to me!" Al boomed, "I need and expect more than some pathetic sorry for this and I'm sorry for that from you. I want you to talk to me and tell me what's going on with you. I'm so tired of walking on eggshells around you!"

"She called here, I was sleep but the ringing of the phone woke me up. I heard a part of your conversation. I could hear the uncertainty in your voice." Veronica paused to look up from the table. Her head had hung in that direction almost the whole time since they sat to eat their meal. "She asked you if you were serious about me, about us. You seemed so hesitant. You never defended me or your choice about us. It hurt. It made me start to think about things."

"What things?" Al was relieved that Veronica was probably expressing her true feelings for him for the first time.

"I was considering how I felt about us; if there was ever going to be or could be an 'us' and I started to feel really good about where we could go from here. That night when I was attacked, all I wanted to do was find a way to get away and get to you. I was more scared about not ever seeing you again than anything that man could have done to harm me."

Al reached across the table and took Veronica's more delicate hands into his own, a quiet assurance that it was fine for her to continue.

"Then that damn phone kept ringing today and so I picked it up to answer it but you'd already done so. I could hear how she was grilling you and how you didn't stand up to her the way I'm so used to hearing from you."

137

Al contemplated Veronica's words and noted how hurt she really was. He also berated him self for causing her any more pain than she already was in. He didn't know how to tell her that she was the source of his uncertainty, that her actions and apparent lack of interest in him romantically had gotten his self-confidence to wane.

"Al, I care about you a great deal, in fact I'm pretty sure I'm in love with you." The words that slipped through Veronica's full lips caused Al's heart to skip a beat. Since the day she walked into his life and offered a cup of coffee to him, Al had been holding his breath to hear those words. He hadn't realized that he was nearly suffocating waiting for her to give her heart to him.

"But Al, if we are going to try and make this work we both have to make some concessions. I have to try to give more of myself to you and you have to learn when to back off and give me my space, agreed?"

"I think I can abide by those terms, but let me ask you one question before we write anything in stone." Al cocked one brow in the air as he waited for Veronica to grant him permission to continue.

"Go on." She conceded with bated breath.

"Did you mean what you just said, about being in love with me?"

Veronica wasn't sure if Al had even heard her due to his lack of response however she knew at that moment that he had heard every word and wanted to hear them again.

There was no sense in trying to retract what she'd said only moments before. Veronica meant every word she'd said and felt blissfully free when she did.

"Yes Al, I meant what I said. I'm in love with you."

Al was speechless. He just stared at Veronica for what could only be described as an extremely uncomfortable period of time before he finally scooped her into his arms and carried Veronica over to the breakfast bar and placed her atop it.

There he silently removed her clothing and began to taste her skin like the Gods themselves had sent him a special blend of nectar. And its name was Veronica. Never had she tasted so sweet, never had he been so ravished and hungered. The more he tried to restrain and pace himself, the more out of control he grew.

The more Veronica's love flowed from her the more he wanted. The louder her cries of ecstasy became, the deeper his primal feeding intensified.

Not once in his young life had Al ever thought that the reciprocated love by another person could cause him such joy, but at the moment of Veronica's profession of love for him, Al began to feel a new person unfold inside him self.

Chapter Sixteen

It was unlike Veronica to make demands of anyone, especially where the opposite sex was concerned, but she'd had enough. Samantha was calling the apartment every day and she was past the point of getting on Veronica's nerves. Veronica truly disliked Samantha Riley and untrustworthy didn't come close to how Veronica described her character.

Al was growing tired of Samantha's antics as well however, to Veronica, he seemed to have the patience of a pre-school teacher with her. Not only was Samantha calling their home at annoying hours and several times a day, but she'd developed a nasty habit of dropping by Four Corners and the Casa offices very frequently. She was always claiming that she had some business to attend to or that she had an exclusive interview that she was conducting. More times than not however, Samantha sat alone, ate alone, or waited in the office lobby for no one to arrive. Once she had fully aggravated either Veronica or whomever she felt comfort in annoying she would make her exit.

On Veronica's first day back to work since the attack two weeks prior, Samantha arrived at the restaurant unannounced and demanded to speak to the director of Sales and Marketing to make arrangements for a group function sponsored by the newspaper.

The moment Landis entered her office; Veronica knew that her day was completely screwed. The look on his face said it all. Samantha Riley was in the building and only a merciful act from God was going to get her to leave without causing a scene.

"She's here", was all Landis said before turning to leave Veronica's office. Veronica genuinely liked Landis he was hard working, easy to get along with, and it didn't hurt that he was easy on the eyes. That smile of his lit up a room and the curly texture of his corn rowed hair only made a woman want to run her fingers through it. Veronica always admired his retreating figure more so than the frontal view because it allowed her the opportunity to glimpse his wonderfully rounded rear.

Landis had a wonderful, graceful physique. He was shorter than Al's height, just an inch or two below six feet, and unlike Al, Landis's weight was centered on his astonishing shoulders. Al's weight was evenly distributed but Landis was obviously a man who worked on his upper body more than anything else on his body. Al had a runners build while Landis looked as if he was a professional boxer.

From the look on his face, Veronica could tell that Landis was not happy with the red-headed siren waiting at the bar. She'd heard him mention on more than one occasion to Al that her antics were growing a bit tiresome and he was tired of having to deal with her, just not as politely. When she'd come to the restaurant to dine, she would go out of her way trying to humiliate him, or anyone who she could get to for that matter. Snapping her fingers at him and constantly, botching his name with horrible substitutions like Land-O-Lakes and Ludwig were some of her milder substitutions.

Veronica pasted the most pleasant expression on her face and mentally prepared herself to go deal with the intolerable Samantha Riley.

"Samantha, it's good to see you again. What can I do for you?" Samantha was days from delivery, so Veronica attempted being as cordial as possible, she was after all with child.

"That's Miss Riley to you." Samantha said tartly.

"My apologies" Veronica offered before continuing "How may I be of service to you? Is this for a function of seventy five people or greater?" The longer the conversation

141

went on the longer Veronica had to pretend to be civil to Samantha, and Veronica's patience was paper thin before the exchange had even begun.

"I doubt that you can handle anything of this magnitude, I mean with your community college education and lack of any type of class, but my editor wants our annual spring social gathering here, you know publicity and all."

Community College education! I hate this woman! Oh God I should have had Landis tell her I wasn't in.

Veronica was effectively blocking out much of what Samantha said until she dared to broach the subject of Veronica's Mother unwed state when she gave birth.

"Excuse me, what did you just say Ms. Riley?" Veronica's biting tone was not lost on Samantha as she managed a smug look of victory.

"I said that you should be able to appeal to many of our more charitable contributors seeing how they love sob stories of little bastard children such as your self." She actually had the gall to repeat it! Veronica wasn't sure if the words or the repetition of the words had floored her more.

Veronica was a little more than shocked by Samantha's outburst. Not only had she managed to hurl more than her allotted share of personal insults during the twenty minutes they had been in each others company, but Samantha had managed to behave as if her words were simple and meant to be complimentary. The truth about it was that Samantha Riley had thoroughly thought out and planned her attack. It was so transparent that it bordered on sad and pitiful. Samantha had resorted to callous and despicable actions. How she managed to gather personal information on Veronica was not a concern. Getting Samantha to leave her place of employment, however, was.

Never in her life had Veronica felt so drained from just being in the presence of another human being but if that was Samantha's goal she had made a stunning effort.

"Ms. Riley I'm so very sorry but I am not feeling very well and unless you would like to continue to work with one of my associates, I'm afraid we'll have to continue another time." Pausing to make sure that her next words gave meaning to Samantha, Veronica continued, "Maybe we can finish the day after tomorrow, say around two. I just can't seem to get rid of this bug in my system and the baby hasn't been very responsive to it either." Veronica began pointedly rubbing her protruding belly.

God help her! She knew that she'd managed to sink to a new low on the catty, feuding, pregnant, bitches roster, but she liked it. In fact Veronica, if she was being honest with herself, had to admit that she absolutely loved the look of disgust and utter mortification on Samantha's face. *God if I had a camera right now I would take the heifer's picture and blow it up and paste it on every billboard in town!*

"Yes well I do understand such things, little Al has been giving me more than a hard time. Had I known that carrying a Carter would be this much trouble I might not have agreed to have my man's baby."

Bitch! Heifer! Cow! Skeezer! Skank! Hoe! Slut! Bitch! Oh wait I already thought of that one. I swear...

Samantha's voice cut through Veronica's personal rant session.

"Yes well I must be going now, I can't make the day after tomorrow so perhaps I can finish this with someone a little more qualified tomorrow, say at around two."

Veronica nodded her head in compliance.

"Good, see you then. You know, you should really find a way to get rid of that bug that's bothering you, I think it may be getting to me as well. Have a good day." With that Samantha left the office without a backwards glance.

Veronica had believed Samantha was capable of a lot of mean and horrible things but never in her life had she ever thought that the woman would walk right into her own place of employment and behave the way she did. Moreover, never had she imagined that the woman would go so far as to suggest that Veronica 'get rid' of her child.

If there was such a thing of Samantha redrawing and crossing a line she'd just done it. Veronica couldn't dial

Al's cell number fast enough on the second ring he answered.

"Hey beautiful, I thought you were only working a half day today?"

"If you want that red-headed bitch to see her twenty-fifth birthday for the fourth time, I suggest you get her together because my being with you did not come with the stipulation that I had to deal with Samantha Riley."

Veronica disconnected the call before Al had a chance to respond.

****

The look of despair on his boss's face said it all to Landis. Al was in a heap load of trouble. He knew once that Samantha woman had shown up at the restaurant again to stir up some mischief, that the fan had started to whirl and was waiting for the loads of crap to hit it.

After Samantha had left the offices at the restaurant Landis could hear Veronica's short but poignant conversation with Al. Landis liked Al and Veronica. In his view people are just people and love knows no color, and while the world, as a whole may not see them that way, he did. Landis had no doubt the two were madly in love, and as he saw it, that was their problem. They were just plain mad.

Landis could look past the fact that they were of different racial background, it really didn't mean two cents to him, but they were crazy. Al had issues with his parents whether he wanted to admit it or not, and Veronica, well with the baby and all the pressure she'd placed on her self not to fail in life and be a victim of circumstance, she had allowed herself to become temperamental. Landis hated to see people his age with such worries about things that should be a delight. He didn't fully understand what was the strain for them. To him having a child should be a joyous occasion, not full of pain and stress. Landis, like most of his co-workers couldn't tell of if there was a joy of impending

144

parenthood from either Al or Veronica. He understood Al's trepidation a bit more though. Al had two children coming at the same time and they were not twins.

Veronica was very stressed. She had valid reason to be completely pissed at Al, but the child she carried did not deserve her ill feelings. Landis, nor anyone else for that matter, thought that Veronica held remorse or ill feeling for her unborn child. She just seemed so unsure. Of what no one really knew, but it was there in her every day. In her stance, the way she walked, talked, even when she went to lunch, she seemed less confident like she was tired and worn, almost defeated.

Landis liked them both, but his personal battle of where his loyalties lay was enough of a concern to make him keep his mouth shut. He wasn't sure if he was on Al's side because he was a man with a sack load of baby mama drama, or if Veronica's cause was his platform. She was after all a black woman who had a lot going for her, and regardless of how smart she was, was dumb enough to get caught up with some man and now a baby. Landis made a choice to just stay out of it, which, he figured, every one else around should do. But knowing how the Carters operated, he was sure everything had yet to hit the fan in the saga of Al and Veronica.

****

Al and Veronica had made amends after her heated explosion on him the day that Samantha came by the restaurant. Veronica had even gained some life and vitality back, but like all good or even semi good things, this all came to an abrupt end when Mariana Sa-Carter stopped by Al's condo unannounced. Al was actually elated that she'd came to visit, she'd never been to Al's home and it was even sweeter that his home had become his and Veronica's.

The doorbell rang around 2:00 in the after noon. It was a Sunday and Al and Veronica had just returned from church. They alternated between his Catholic Church and her Missionary Baptist, it was her week and hence the late hour of release from worship.

"You expecting someone?" he asked.

"Yeah, Renee was supposed to come by for dinner, but not until six" she answered confused as to why Renee would come by so early. Renee was late for her own birth by two weeks and had not been on time for anything since, let alone actually early.

"I'll get it" Veronica announced, but Al ran up to her and nudged her back into her seat. Veronica was only around six and a half months pregnant and simple tasks had become such a chore for her, besides no matter what she tried to do, Al found a way to get her out of it and do it for her instead, she would muse to herself that if he could find a way to pee twenty times a day for her, he would.

Al dashed over to the intercom and pressed the talk button.

"Yes?"

"Alejandro, it's your mother." Came the distinguished sounding clipped English. Even though she had resided in the States for more than thirty years, Mariana had not lost her accent to the American flow of common tongue. Mariana spoke fluent English when her and Simon Sr. had met in Brazil, but she had yet to lose that lovely accent of hers. Not quite Spanish or French it seemed to be a little of both with a little Dutch mixed in at times, it was sexy but more over it was endearing, just like it's possessor.

"Mama, Come in." Al buzzed her in and left the condo to greet his mother at the elevator. The doorman only worked during weekdays and on certain hours so it was his off day and the tenants and their guest found their way around with out him. Veronica was a nervous wreck. Nausea was ensuing quickly but her bloated body would not permit her to move fast enough and she just tried to make due and breathe slowly. She only met Al's mother once and it was very quickly and in passing. She seemed demure

146

enough to be a Carter wife, but the meeting only really amounted to a quick hello and light shaking of hands.

Mariana entered the apartment first with Al right behind in tow.

"Mama, you remember Veronica Parker?" he said while removing her jacket.

"I do" was her cool response. From that moment Veronica's stomach churning turned to a title wave.

"Mrs. Carter, A pleasure to see you again" Veronica said addressing the mother of the man she loved. It was blatantly obvious where Al had gotten his looks. Mariana was tall and slender with sandy brown hair and vibrant green eyes. Al was a mirror image of her despite the fact that his eyes were blue and his hair was much darker, attributes that he'd inherited from his father.

"Well we'll see about all of that, won't we?" Al's surprise at his Mother's attitude was lost on Veronica. Her own shock didn't allow her to see it. Not to be put off by Mariana Carter, grandmother of her child or not, Veronica questioned what she meant by the comment.

"I mean exactly that, my dear. I don't mean to come here and cause a disturbance, but there are some things that I need to clear up for myself"

"And what would those things be, Mama?" Al interceded before Veronica could respond.

"Well, like for instance, Son." She said emphasizing the word "Son", "When is the mother of your child due?"

"Veronica is expect…" Al was cut off by his Mother.

"I mean Samantha, Alejandro. She is carrying your child as well, isn't she?"

"I suppose you're right, but I'll wait until after the child is born and a paternity is done before I draw conclusions." Al's conviction was strong but Mariana's was unshakable.

"That is just fine of you, but what about her" she said nodding her head towards Veronica.

Veronica felt like she was watching a tennis match.

"What do you mean what about her, and by the way she does have a name"

"I mean you aren't going to get a paternity test for that child as well?"

"Why should I?"

"Because, where women are concerned, you've seemed to be a bit careless No offense Veronica" Mariana said with a slight glance at Veronica.

"None taken" Veronica stated. She was truly in no way offended.

"Mama, I want you to apologize to Veronica this very moment."

"Al, it's okay. She has no reason to apologize" Veronica interjected. Veronica really didn't like the tone Mrs. Carter had taken, but she was right. Veronica was reluctant to get involved with Al because of all the drama that came along with him. If she enumerated everything, things seemed a bit impossible. One, she was pregnant out of wed lock, two, she was pregnant out of wed lock by a man who had a child on the way by another woman, three, she was pregnant by her boss, and there were other issues that she could have tacked on but she figured what was the point, the first three were enough.

"No, Veronica. I do owe you an apology." Mariana offered to bewildered Veronica. "I apologize to you for all of the mess that Alejandro has gotten you into. I know that you care about him deeply and that he cares for you, but I must question if that care is deep enough for you to put so much on the line."

"What do you mean?" Al and Veronica asked in unison.

"I mean, you both are young, but you my dear," Mariana said to Veronica, "are younger and less acquainted with life and all its ups and downs than my son. He not only has one but two women pregnant, at the same time I might add, and is not married to either one. This by the way is not looked upon very well with his family. Let's not forget that he is your employer and this cannot serve your reputation positively, and unless you plan on trying to find a new job in a new town, word will travel well. Shall I continue?" Mariana, as usual was accurate in her appraisal of the situation.

"Well. Mrs. Carter, what would you like for me to do? I'm not going to quit my job and I believe that my work is well enough for the company not to fire me. I broke no rules, and have done no wrong to the company, the Carter name, or your son. I love him and our child and I'm not willing to compromise those things for anything." Al sat opposite the women that he loved astonished. Until that point Veronica had seemed unsure and confused about their future. However, at that moment she began to show him her guts and willingness to fight for them. She showed that she believed that they were worth fighting for. At that very moment he knew that Veronica Parker was going to be the one and only Mrs. Alejandro Carter.

"I don't want you to do anything, Veronica. And I mean that with all sincerity. I believe that you are one of the most competent and talented people I've come across in this business."

"Thank you for the compliment but I wasn't fishing for one. Frankly I don't need your or anyone else's validation of my work. No offense."

Mariana smiled at the ending remark "Touché. I never thought that you did. I just hope that the both of you are prepared for the battle ahead of you. I've never claimed to like Samantha and truthfully, I don't know much about you Veronica to draw conclusions about you personally. All I know is that you don't rub me the wrong way, and I know my Alejandro is completely in love with you."

"Mama, I can convey my own feelings for Veronica" Al said with flushed cheeks.

Mariana looked at her son and let out a big sigh. The entire room was quiet as all three occupants sat deep in their own thoughts. Mariana's thoughts taking her to a place of worry for her son and his love, that any concerned parent would have. Veronica was a truly remarkable woman to get Al to settle down and fight so vigorously for what they had.

Veronica's thoughts had gone to her life and where it was in relation to where she'd anticipated it being at that point. She thought that she'd be putting in long hours at her new job, building an illustrious career in the restaurant and hospitality industry. There was no room for a man and definitely no thought of a child. But she wouldn't give up anything as it was for what she previously thought she wanted.

Al's mind was a jumble of everything. He'd yet to tell Sam of his intentions of getting a paternity test and consequently he'd yet to tell Veronica of his not asking. All Al wanted in his life was Veronica, but some how he hadn't done the things necessary for that to happen. Sure she was living with him but he didn't feel very secure about that, and that was mainly his own doing. All the while he was asking Veronica for some kind of commitment, he was not giving her the same in return. He'd asked her to give him her all, no holding back; and he'd yet to reciprocate the same to her.

His biggest fear would come true if he didn't take action soon. Veronica was a very smart and practical young lady, and even though she loved him, Al knew that she'd leave that love behind before she let him trample on her feelings.

****

"Samantha, there's a call for you. It's Alejandro Carter"

"Tell him I'm busy and that I'll call him later."

Al had made a vow to himself that he would make things right for him and Veronica. He wanted everything for them and for their unborn child. They finally decided to find out the sex of the child, a girl. The thought disturbed him that some selfish man could do horrible things to his own daughter. Or in the case of the child Samantha was soon to deliver, his son could turn out to be that selfish man to do less than honorable actions against an unworthy female victim.

Al would call Samantha at home and get the answering machine, call the cell phone, get the voice mail, or call her at work and get the receptionist telling him that she was too busy to take his call. He'd had enough and his patience was beyond the point of worn out. Grabbing his umbrella, Al headed out his office set on making Samantha speak to him. If she was unwilling to take his call then she'd see him.

****

Time had gone by so quickly for Veronica. She was just a few months away from delivering her baby, a girl. She and Al had decided to name her Selena Rai. Actually Al had come up with the name one day while they were out and about town. They were looking for baby clothes and decided to stop for a bite to eat in the Coventry area. Veronica adored the street that ran through a near by east side suburb. On one three block strip of street one could find their hearts desire. Between fun little boutiques to vinyl record stores that sold vintage albums there was more than enough to keep a persons mind, body, and spirit full.

Al and Veronica had decided to eat at a vegetarian restaurant. Since Veronica had entered her later months of pregnancy she'd been having difficulty keeping meat products down. They were enjoying a shared plate of grilled eggplant with marinara sauce when Al broached the subject of baby names.

"Well, what would you like to call her?" the question came out of left field. Veronica was steadily concentrating on eating all of her food when He posed the inquiry.

"I hadn't given it much thought to be honest. I was planning on letting the sex be a surprise."

"What does that have to do with the name?" he asked a little confused by her response.

151

"Well I kind of wanted everything to just come. I mean when the baby is born I just wanted to pick a name that fits her."

"Understandable and admirable even, sorry if I ruined that for you. I really wanted to know."

Veronica smiled at Al with all the love and admiration that she felt for him. "I know you wanted to know. That's why I said okay to the doctor during the ultra sound"

"You did that for me?"

"Yes, why wouldn't I? It's not the end of the world to know and if that's what makes you happy, I'm okay with it"

"Wow, I had no clue" Al was touched by her selfless gesture. He had no idea how she felt about the whole thing and that she'd be willing to put her wants to the side for him. The thought of it made his heart stretch a little wider so that Veronica could get more comfortable there.

"What about Jasmine?" Veronica said breaking Al's musings.

"I could count the Jasmine's I know on two sets of hands"

"Interesting, I didn't know you frequented the opposite sex so much." Veronica said with a smirk. Al winced at his mistake but decided against taking the conversation any closer to that subject.

"What about naming her after one of our mothers and giving the other mother's name as a middle name."

"Alejandro please, I will not have our parents fighting over who our child gets named after."

"Good Point" they both sat silent for a few moments when Al blurted out "Selena Rai"

Veronica sat silent while toying with the name inside her head. The Selena she liked but the "Ray" she was uncertain about and she told Al as much.

"Not R-A-Y but R-A-I" he stated with a goofy school- boy grin on his face.

"Why that name?"

"Well Selena because I loved her music and I believed she died before her time and Rai because I had a childhood friend named Rey, R-E-Y who passed from a terrible accident when I was nine. I guess the two just fit together" Al's grin didn't reach his sad eyes and Veronica understood and would not push him for details about Rey.

"Selena Rai it is."

****

The smile on Al's face from the memory of naming his child dissipated like water in the desert sands when Samantha Riley appeared into his view.

He hadn't noticed before how unappealing Samantha really was to him. What he once thought as great long legs now had an "Olive Oil" feel to them. He once thought her breast pert and cute in size, but upon further consideration her breasts were barely there. With the pregnancy Samantha may have grown to a b cup, but that was pushing it. Al had to admit to himself that Samantha was attractive in her own right. Her Irish red hair, freckles, and those emerald green eyes could make any red blooded male quiver from the sight of her.

Even with all of the things he found attractive about her, Al couldn't help comparing his very recent past to his present and what he hoped as his future. Veronica possessed something about her that was hard to translate into English text. She didn't have the height like Sam nor did she have some of the other attributes Sam had that Al had once found attractive. Veronica had a grace and sweetness that was beyond compare. She had a smile that was gleaming and, not that she tried for any other affect, pure. As far as the subject of body shape, Veronica had curves that the finest European engineer would have trouble inventing a contraption to navigate. Her breasts were full and soft, womanly, her hips ample and pleasing to the touch. Her skin smooth like the milk chocolate it's tone reminded one of. Veronica was the woman of Al's dreams that he didn't know he was dreaming about.

The woman who stood before him at that moment was quickly becoming a nightmare.

"Alejandro, to what do I owe this pleasure?" Samantha asked with a contrite smile.

"Is there some place that we can talk privately, Samantha?" Al was beyond pleasantries.

"Well, I was on my way out but I suppose if you don't mind me riding along, we can talk in the cab over to the hospital. I'm past due and the doctor is considering inducing labor. Al hadn't paid much attention to Sam's pregnancy, but if she'd told him the truth she was more than a week beyond her due date.

"What ever Sam, let's go then."

Driving East bound through the now summer influenced streets of Cleveland, Al and Samantha sat in silence waiting for the traffic signal to change. Then an almost barely audible voice broke the air.

"Samantha, I want a paternity test."

"What!" shock evident on Samantha's features.

"You heard me. There's no need in arguing this point because without one your child will remain fatherless. I will not sign the birth certificate and any money that you try to get from me will be disputed until paternity is proven." The void of emotion frightened Al.

He was completely over Sam. She'd used him as a pawn to attempt to obtain what she wanted from him and his family name. She never really cared about him as a person. All she wanted from him was the stature that being with him could afford her. She's Samantha Riley and he Alejandro Carter. Together they would have been not just Cleveland's but the states new young power couple.

"What happened to us Al? We were so good for each other." Al noted the hint of remorse in Sam's voice and thought *she has a lot of goddamn nerve!*

"On that point you are so mistaken. We were never good for or to each other. I used you and you used me. I wanted company. And you wanted someone with enough clout to forward your career."

154

Samantha's face didn't mirror her embarrassment. While she hated Al's words she couldn't deny them. He was right but she was not going to let things go that easily.

"Screw you! I was in this for the long haul. I guess you've clearly laid out what you were in for; free ass from me. You know what you are? A coward, a yellow-bellied coward. You use people and when they catch on to your little game you throw blame elsewhere. Why don't you act like a man for once in your life, Alejandro?"

They had reached their destination. Al slowed and pulled in front of the large modern structure. The hospital was Cleveland's largest and one of the country's best, and was housed in one of the cities newest and biggest structures. It wasn't tall like the building that four Corners were located in, but it spanned a few blocks.

Al turned his solemn face on Samantha. Without another word she exited the car and with all the dignity she could muster walked towards the hospital entry. Not another word was spoken to Al, nor was another thought given to Samantha that day.

Al returned home much later that day. His mouth watered at the smell of Veronica's cooking. He could tell she'd made a real soul food dinner. The smell of chicken and candied yams greeted him at the door. To be honest Al had never really had a real soul food dinner before Veronica cooked one for him weeks prior. She'd made pork chops, collard greens, black eyed peas, and hot water corn bread. Al swore he'd died and gone to heaven.

Al stood in the kitchen entry for almost a minute before Veronica turned and acknowledged him.

"I see you've decided to grace us with your presence" She said rubbing her now enormous belly.

"I think everyone present would have to admit grace is not something I have an abundance of"

"How was your day?" Veronica hadn't been to work. She was experiencing labor pains too early and the Doctor ordered her to take it easy.

With a reflective sigh and crooked smile he said "This has been one of the longest days of my life, but now that I'm here with you, it's ending way too soon."

Epilogue

One Year Later:

Veronica barely let the sedan come to a complete stop before she hopped out the car and ran up the stairs to her home. She and Al had bought the four bedroom Colonial 3 months prior. She'd been away from her family almost a week and couldn't wait to hold her daughter in her arms and kiss her husband.

With some reluctance Veronica agreed to marry Al. She made him agree to one stipulation that he was still struggling to fulfill: be civil and polite to Samantha. Granted Samantha didn't help situations. She would cancel on Al and Veronica when he was scheduled to pick up his son, call and say that she needed money, for the baby, and try to get Al to come over without his wife. It was very trying for the newly-weds.

Getting Samantha to agree to a paternity test was a battle in and of itself. Samantha hadn't wanted to admit that there may be another father, but when Al pushed for a test she confessed that there was another possible father. Apparently while she was involved with Al she'd been carrying on with one of the Mayor's assistants. However as Avery grew there was no mistaking Paternity, He was a spitting image of his father, including the cobalt blue eyes. The only feature Avery had gotten from his mother was her pale coloring and freckles. It made for a very striking combination on the child, and would no doubt garner him a lot of attention from the opposite sex.

"Al! I'm back!" Veronica bellowed as she entered the front door.

"Shhhh!" Al cautioned with his sleeping child in his arms on the sofa. Veronica had become lovelier since the birth of the baby. Her hips, if at all possible, became rounder and fuller and her skin glowed like the sun just before sunset on a long summer's night. It was hot, intense, and full of wonder.

"Sorry," she whispered as she sat next to the two most important people in her life. "I'm just so happy to be home"

"How was the conference?" Veronica had been asked to attend and present at a convention for African American Hospitality Professionals.

"Great, we'll talk about that later" smiling Veronica removed her pumps and grabbed her daughter from her husband.

There was something about the scene that warmed Al to his core. Never had he thought his life could be so complete. Even though he had conflict with Samantha, he'd never felt so at peace.

For all of her shortcomings, Samantha gave Al the best advice he'd ever received. He'd behaved as a Man and protected and took care of the persons he loved, his wife and children. He had made peace with himself. He made a vow to make things right for Veronica, and there was no other place that she wanted to be but with him. Life was a work in progress for them, but when finished, He prayed that it was to be the greatest masterpiece ever made.

The End

A Note from the Author:

Thank you for taking this journey with me in the lives of Alejandro and Veronica Carter. This story is one of personal growth and love that developed between the two. I hope the characters are as real to you as they are to me.

I soon hope to bring you the continuing story from many of the characters you've met. I hope we meet again in the pages of these wonderful and intriguing persons lives.

Until Then,
D. E. Arrington
Contact: de@dearrington.com